THE KNOWING

THE KNOWING
MADELEINE RYAN

SCRIBE

Melbourne | London | Minneapolis

Scribe Publications
18–20 Edward St, Brunswick, Victoria 3056, Australia
2 John St, Clerkenwell, London, WC1N 2ES, United Kingdom
3754 Pleasant Ave, Suite 100, Minneapolis, Minnesota 55409, USA

Published by Scribe 2025

Typeset in Portrait by the publishers

Printed and bound in the UK by CPI Group (UK) Ltd,
Croydon CR0 4YY

Scribe is committed to the sustainable use of natural resources and
the use of paper products made responsibly from those resources.

Scribe acknowledges Australia's First Nations peoples as the
traditional owners and custodians of this country, and we pay
our respects to their elders, past and present.

978 1 761380 19 8 (Australian edition)
978 1 915590 13 8 (UK edition)
978 1 761385 80 3 (ebook)

Catalogue records for this book are available from the
National Library of Australia and the British Library.

scribepublications.com.au
scribepublications.co.uk
scribepublications.com

for our mothers' dreams

When Camille realised she'd forgotten her phone, she wanted to cry.

Not immediately. Not when she saw it in her mind's eye at home on the charger. At that point, she was still deluded enough to think she could salvage the situation. She seriously thought she might have enough time to drive back to the house, and to get it, and to return to the train station, and to maybe get a takeaway coffee, and to settle into a seat in the Quiet Carriage.

The clock in the car is broken and Camille doesn't wear a watch. She knew the train was leaving at 8.06am, as it does every weekday morning, and that the clock in the car said 7.56am. She just had no idea whether the clock in the car was running five or ten minutes fast. It used to be ten, and then, not that long ago, Camille noticed it was catching up. But she knew that the drive from the train station to the house takes four minutes, because she once listened to a song, she can't remember which one, and it was exactly four minutes long, and it got her from the house to the station. So she would've needed at least eight minutes to get home and back. Then thirty-seconds-to-a-minute to enter the house, and to yell over her shoulder at Manny, and to jump around the dogs, and to unplug and grab her phone, and to run out of the house again, before hopping back into the car and becoming a hazard to everyone and everything. Then she would've needed up to three minutes to find a new parking space, and perhaps another two minutes to race to the platform, and it all would've been too much, just too fucking much.

Commuters were swarming through the parking lot: in cars, on foot, via bus, with bikes. She could've asked someone for the exact time. It's just that, realistically, if she had actually stopped and done that, like, if she had actually stopped the car, or chosen to get out of the car, or chosen to yell at a complete stranger from the car, and then proceeded to deal with all of the nuances of an interaction with a person she might then be forced to see every other weekday morning on Platform One — after the whole, 'Hey! Yeah! I want to be nice! Even though I don't have time! And, ah, yeah, *WHAT'S THE TIME*? Quickly! No need to smile! No need to comment on anything! The weather is the same! It's the weather! Let it go! Let it do its thing! And, yes, it's Valentine's Day! Happy happy! Don't look at me! Don't think! Just answer!' incident — she would've run out of time altogether. And she couldn't catch the next train, because it only gets to Southern Cross Station fifteen minutes before she's supposed to be at work, and there's still another twenty-minute train ride from Southern Cross to Armadale, and she simply couldn't be late for that.

Or for Holly.

Camille wrestled with the 9am start Holly 'deeply preferred' for more than a year and she couldn't handle it. The earlier train arrived at Armadale so long before 9am that she'd find herself suspended in this disorienting half an hour of nothingness before the day with Holly even began.

Then Camille started questioning things and reflecting upon things, after having spent more than eighty minutes on the train trying to avoid questioning things and reflecting upon things, and she had to go through this process five times a week, every week, and sometimes even more times a week when some star-studded event, or party, or wedding, or bat mitzvah required more of Holly! And more of Camille! And more of Alyce! And more of Georgia! And more of the flowers! And all the world's flowers!

Yet despite Camille's fears and dramas, she did actually manage to ask Holly if she would be willing to push the starting time of their day forward an hour to 10am.

And Holly said yes.

But even thinking about that whole ordeal puts Camille into fight-or-flight mode again. Asking Holly for anything is a ferocious trauma, and there isn't enough marijuana or ashwagandha on the planet to get Camille through it. She lives in a state of recovering from, anticipating, or inadvertently managing to activate conflict with Holly, and then bending over backwards to try and diffuse it. Camille doesn't know why, but this pattern seems to run her life, along with clocks, seasons, invoices, diagnostics, the threat of fine lines, and everyone else's desires.

And thanks to her now being phone-less, she cannot distract herself from these intolerable aspects of her humanness. She can't scroll any feeds. She can't watch any instructional vids. She can't laugh at any memes. She can't put any bottles of limited-edition botanical perfume or boxes of hand-rolled incense sticks in a shopping cart and forget about them. She can't look at any sponsored posts from 'it' girls sailing across the Mediterranean in spangly bikinis and being sexy-yet-candid in hotel rooms. She can't read any reviews of restaurants she'll never eat at, because her diet is plant-based, yet she'll obsess over the way they describe those crackling pulled-pork sandwiches, and those oily anchovy-and-garlic pizzas, and those sweet, sticky egg-noodle dishes. She can't listen to any music. She can't send Manny any funny gifs about Valentine's Day because she doesn't. Have. Her. Phone.

Camille has been wanting to read books on the train to give her eyes a rest, and to give her insecurities a rest, and to give her soul a rest, but she hasn't gotten around to it, because there are so many things she needs to do on her phone first. Maybe she'll buy a book in the city on the way home, and the prospect of that is comforting. Although, she'd like to research different books online before buying one, and she can't.

So Camille's holding back tears as she finds a seat on the peak-hour train that never has enough carriages to comfortably space everybody out, and she wants everything to stop, and she wants to turn around, and to go back, and to change course, but the train she's on is leaving the station, and propelling her deeper into herself; deeper into all of the places she'd rather not go.

Camille doesn't have any money now, either. There were a couple of travel cards in the glove box of the car, but they're Manny's concession cards, and Camille isn't eligible for a concession. She's just hoping no ticket inspectors board the train, and she has no idea how she's going to get through the suspense of it all, or how she's going to pay for a coffee, or for her lunch, or for anything else that comes up throughout the day. She's probably going to have to ask Holly for help.

Camille just laughed out loud. Well, she kind of snorted out loud into the void of the shared public space, and no one noticed, because they were all looking at their phones.

Camille had been super preoccupied with charging her phone yesterday, too. She'd wanted the thing powering up overnight, but Manny wouldn't let her do it. He didn't want it plugged in so close to them while they were sleeping. In fact, he didn't want the phone charging anywhere in the house at all overnight, which Camille totally gets. She's just not sure how that differs from when they're charging their devices during the day. But anyway. Manny must feel more exposed to predators during the night and that fear is, like, projected onto the phone? Or something?

As a rule, Manny's fears tend toward the practical — 'lock the doors at night' and 'we're not walking the dogs through the long grass because *snakes*' and 'keep your wallet on you in case you *lose or forget your phone*' and 'the old man didn't top up my bank account' — while Camille's fears tend toward the social and the spiritual. Like, 'I think she's acting this way to discourage me from asking for a promotion' and 'they're pissed off because it's our turn to have them over for dinner' and 'if you believe in your work, others will, too.' Camille has repeated this last statement to Manny many times, and he hasn't really taken it in, because she hasn't really taken it in.

Camille wants to believe in the work she does at her job, but she doesn't. Because the work Camille does at her job isn't something to be believed in, it's something to be done, because Holly's told her to do it. Camille is yet to do work that will *consume* her. Oh, the pleasure of being *consumed* by something. Camille doesn't have that. So she's consumed by everyone and everything else.

Therefore, it's pretty rich for her to tell Manny to believe in his work. The notion that 'you teach best what you have yet to learn' may be popular, but you can't teach what you don't know, and you can never really explain what you do know. But more on that later.

And Camille's phone was on 42% when she and Manny went to bed last night, and she didn't know whether thirty-five minutes of charging as she got dressed this morning would give it enough juice to last all day. And she didn't want to take the charger to work, because Manny might need it at home, and they only have one. Until recently, they'd had two, but Charger Number Two vanished under mysterious circumstances involving a friend of Manny's who'd stayed with them for a few weeks. Friend of Manny's didn't bring his own charger, and he abruptly vacated the premises after an incident involving sugary homemade donuts, and weed, and a reluctance to contribute to the cost of groceries, and a friend's party that he wanted to go to in Melbourne, right around the time Charger Number Two went MIA. But look. Camille would probably lose a charger if she took it into the city, anyway. Because that's what happens to everything that goes into the city. It gets lost. And Camille would never ask Holly for a charger once she gets to work, because Camille doesn't like to ask Holly for anything, ever.

Whenever Camille needs something, Holly gets this look in her eyes. It's as if she's taking a photo of the moment when Camille was vulnerable, and she'll remind her of it, directly or indirectly, during another moment, when she is asking Camille for something completely outrageous, and Camille is hesitant for a second, and then *BOOM*. Holly will turn whatever she's asking for in this future, hypothetical scenario into an equivalent scenario, even though any reasonable person can see that it isn't an equivalent scenario. It's an irrational scenario. Yet in this future, hypothetical, irrational scenario, Camille will feel bad, and she will give in to Holly's demands, and she'll quickly hand over whatever Holly wants, because she feels chronically spineless in Holly's presence, which is surprising, because Camille has an air of genuine competency about her that puts others at ease. But, right now, Camille believes herself to be at the mercy of Holly's every whim. So she is at the mercy of Holly's every whim. Hence why Camille concluded that asking Holly for a charger once she got to work would be a no-no and that charging the phone for thirty-five minutes this morning would be enough. And it was. It's just that Camille then proceeded to forget the phone altogether. She even checked how it was going five minutes before leaving the house, and it was roaring along at 89%, which is where it has stayed. Frozen in time, at 89%.

The idea of it sitting there on top of her dad's old record player makes her stomach twist, and her jaw clench, and her brow furrow, and then she remembers not to furrow her brow, because she doesn't want wrinkles.

What concerns Camille the most is how freakishly calm she'd been on the drive from her house to the station. It didn't feel like she had forgotten anything. She was so relaxed and prepared for the day ahead. Even the idea of dealing with Holly didn't perturb her as much as it usually might. There was a silence inside her, and it was calming. The weekend had been so replenishing: cleaning, walking the dogs, smelling the eucalyptus trees after the rain, going to the market, falling asleep on Manny in front of a foreign film about friendship. Maybe it was finally time to surrender to the hours, to the demands, to the job, to the Holly.

Last night, Camille checked the weather forecast, which said the temperature today was going to be cool in the morning and then reach a high of twenty-eight degrees. There might be a bit of rain early on and a bit of sun later. So Camille laid out a black linen mini-dress, and black unisex Doc Martens, and black ankle socks. Black, black, black, and black. Always black.

No bra. Black cotton undies. She packed her black keep-cup, and her black menstrual cup, and she painted her nails black, and she put her headphones in the front pocket of her black messenger bag, and she gazed through the bedroom window at the full super moon in Aquarius against the black sky. Super, super full. Low. Yellow. A whole other world. Right there.

Then, in the morning, while Manny was asleep, Camille commenced The Morning Routine. She washed and double-conditioned her hair before leaving it to air-dry. It's long and blonde. She wants to cut it, because she thinks she'll feel more purposeful with it short. Kind of like how she thought she'd feel more sensual if it were long.

She shaved her underarms, and her legs, and she had mixed feelings about this, as she always does. Camille tells herself that she'd prioritise smoothness whether Manny was in her life or not, but she also knows that the feeling of his hands moving up and down her shaved and moisturised legs is something she relishes about living this life, in this body.

Then, in the process of wrapping a towel around herself, Camille caught a glimpse of her nakedness in the bathroom mirror, and she didn't even see her naturally toned legs, her high cheekbones, her oval eyes, her full lips. Camille prefers to focus on what she lacks: big boobs, toned muscles. The latter could be developed. The former would have to be bought. And she didn't think about the thick scar that cuts through her right eyebrow, because it's become akin to an unusual landmark, which she's gotten used to because she lives near it.

Camille acquired The Scar when she was eleven. Her family went on a trip along the Great Ocean Road, and while running around Lorne's rock pools and feeling stimulated by the new place, Camille tripped. She can still remember the bright-red blood spreading gracefully through the nearby pool of water. She couldn't believe it came from her. Camille passed out, and the next thing she remembers is being on the sand, flat on her back, looking up at the sky. Smelling seawater. Feeling cold, feeling different. Like something had happened to her while she was unconscious, and that the big blue up above was less like something outside of her and more like a part of her.

But, this morning, none of this crossed Camille's mind as she spritzed her face with aloe vera and rosewater face mist, and as she slathered her extremities in shea butter, and got dressed. She contemplated wearing sunscreen and decided against it. Surely it wouldn't be needed. She'd hardly be outside. Then Camille remembered all those articles and podcasts about how crucial sunscreen is year-round. One dermatologist insisted that sunscreen was important at *all times*. Even *indoors*. I mean, hello. Like, WINDOWS. But Camille hates the way sunscreen feels on her skin and what the incessant application of it implies about being alive and on the earth — as if being touched by the sun was inherently dangerous and unnatural.

Camille doesn't wear make-up, either. What you see is what you get, morning, noon, and night. She used to wear it — some bronzer here, some mascara there — but she started to freak out about the ingredients. Then Manny told her that he hated make-up, because it was 'phony', and she couldn't really argue with him, so she stopped using it.

But, one day after work, Camille went into a cosmetics store in Armadale to buy another gardenia candle, and one of the bored members of staff roaming the shop floor offered to give her a makeover. Camille said ok, but no make-up. Just oils. Serums. Maybe a toning water? The attendant looked perplexed and then found himself walking a fine line between wanting to make a sale, telling Camille off, calling her ugly, and trying to make her feel beautiful, because, like, what about those bags under your eyes, babe? Don't you want some concealer? And what about that uneven skin tone? Don't you want some foundation? Or tinted moisturiser? And what about the lines that are going to deepen around your eyes? And mouth? Don't you want some caffeinated plumper? And what about those freckles? And all of that melasma? *SURELY YOU WANT SUNSCREEN?*

Camille patiently said no, no, and no, before almost putting a $180 hydrating face cream she didn't need on a payment plan, and exiting the premises clutching her gardenia candle, which is now burning atop her dresser drawers as she gets ready: a reminder of timeless beauty and sensuality. A reminder that she's more than this day, this job. A reminder that she's an open flame.

Then Camille put on night-blooming-jasmine perfume. She applied it to her wrists, and to both sides of her neck, and she placed the small bottle in her pocket, not yet knowing how instrumental it would become in the hours ahead.

She moved to the kitchen and toasted a thick piece of sourdough from what was left of the loaf she and Manny'd bought from the old guy with the moustache and the striped apron at the weekend market. She then rubbed it with a clove of garlic and drizzled it with cold-pressed olive oil, before preparing a whole avocado, which was perfectly ripe. *Perfectly.* The flesh came out of the skin easily, as if the gods knew it was to be consumed at that exact moment. Then Camille mashed it, and squeezed lemon through it, and licked her fingers. She piled the mountain of avo atop the bread and put it on a plate, which would sit on the passenger seat of the car until she arrived at the station. And Camille could see her future self, standing on Platform One, headphones in, music playing, holding that piece of decadence in one hand, and taking an enormous bite from it as she waited for the train. As she waited for duty, and obligation, to devour her.

And as Camille was getting into the car with her plate, she sensed the quality of the air, and she inhaled a bit deeper. She rarely notices the world around her when she's going into the city. It's, like, a peripheral thing. But on the drive to the station this morning, Camille saw the world around her as a wonder waiting to be discovered.

So she rolled the windows down, and she looked at the trees, and she admired their enormous trunks. She wondered about everything they had seen: the seasons, the roadworks, the gold-diggers — literally, the area used to be goldfields — the accidents, the residents and their descendants. Then the reality of her own transience became overwhelming, and she returned her attention to the white lines of the road.

Manny's Placebo CD was still in the player from when they'd washed the car together the night before, and you know what? When Camille realised that she had forgotten her phone, she considered not going into the city at all. Yep. Maybe it was a sign. If Manny had been in the car with her, he definitely would've told her not to go.

Like, definitely.

Manny and Camille met at a really foul party. Actually, they met at a series of foul parties hosted by mutual friends that were scattered across Melbourne during one summer, years ago. Some of these festy occasions were costume parties. Some of them weren't. Some of them were drug-fuelled and some of them weren't. None of them were kinky.

The parties Manny and Camille attended smelled, and felt, like sweaty Australian garbage. Every night, the air was thick with haze. The days had been overcast, and the nights were muggy. Everyone was thirsty for a good time, but unwilling to contribute anything other than their own needy filth and grime to any given social situation. It was all like, 'hey, can we share that ride?' And 'are you getting the slab this time?' And 'did you get a pic of that?' And 'yeah, I quit, but. Umm. Okayyyyy, I'll have some!' And 'so who's going, anyway?'

Camille thought Manny was arrogant, and Manny thought Camille was a poser. Things were pretty straightforward initially. But then one night, a group of them went down to the beach. They'd been at a toga party, which involved lots of white bedsheets, flower garlands, stubbies, daisy chains, laurel wreaths, and sunburn. It had been in a Victorian terrace house on Beaconsfield Parade, which is a wide road alongside the beach, lined with palm trees. It has a promenade overlooking the sea, and the city, and the shipping docks, and plenty of sand leading down to the water.

The terrace house was owned by an ex-private school boy's parents, which is often the case with terrace houses in Melbourne. And much to Camille's delight, its courtyard garden was overflowing with native and exotic flowers, vines, fruit trees, and vegetables, because the ex-private school boy stumbled upon a pile of 1960s *Women's Weekly Gardening* magazines at St Kilda Market for five bucks. So he brought them home and instead of writing them off as novelty items to impress others with, or putting them in the dunny, he actually read them. Not only did he read them, but he applied their homely wisdom. And behold. Paradise.

It was a full moon in Scorpio.

Eight partygoers ventured down to the beach.

One of them was a friend of Camille's, Lily, who was at the party with her long-term boyfriend, Tom. They were, and are, graphic designers that have since moved to Berlin and had a baby, because of course they did, and of course they have. In Lily's most recent email to Camille, she was like, 'we're actually thinking of moving to Norway because they're way more chill when it comes to working and having babies and stuff.'

It was after midnight. Everyone was sifting around on the sand drinking, and smoking, and threatening to go into the water and then refusing to do so. Manny arrived on the last tram of the night, claiming to have come from another party. He was dressed in his usual black Levi's and a self-conscious, worn-out black cotton T-shirt, with heavy closed-toed black Birkenstocks, which he spent way too much time insisting were 'totally in accordance' with the night's theme.

No one cares, dude. No one cares, Camille thought.

It turned out Manny had come all the way from his Brunswick share house, and he'd had to rush, because he'd spent hours stressing about what to wear, and texting his mate Liam, who was already at the party, about whether making the trek was worth the effort. And good ol' Liam had dutifully taken time out of his night to reply to Manny with enthusiastic 'hell yeahs' and starry-eyed emojis before a few 'get down here!!!'s and, as the exchange wore on, some earnest 'maybe come now-ish?' sentiments, before he was asked to list the party's current attendees, in detail, and Manny felt funny when Liam said, 'and that blonde chick with The Scar.' So Manny made haste.

And while everyone was indulging Manny's antics, it occurred to Camille that she really did want to go into the water. The only problem was that Camille had nothing on underneath her toga. She regretted that seemingly liberated 6pm decision. Her private rebellion was now shackling her to the shore. Half of the people on the beach were her friends. Surely it was ok to go into the water naked? It was her world, too. It was her body's world. Couldn't she enjoy it without worrying that people will think she's an attention-seeking slut trying to show off her bod?

And as she was contemplating the ins-and-outs of this, she heard a voice. It said, 'I'll go in with you.' Then Camille turned around and saw this creature. This vulnerable, quite possibly stupid, but maybe insightful, and actually quite handsome creature, trying to connect with her. There was a look of curiosity and fear in his eyes. And she liked it.

'I'm kind of naked.'

'Literally or metaphorically?'

'Well, I'm not wearing anything under my toga.'

'Just go in in the toga?'

'Really?'

'Yes? It's, like, a zillion degrees. It'll dry in two seconds.'

'Ok.'

'Ok.'

Camille threw off her toga as she entered the water, and didn't look back. Manny followed in his black Calvin Klein boxers, feeling pumped that he'd put on designer undies, because they were the only clean pair he could find, and they didn't have any holes. *Nice.*

The two of them acclimatised to the temperature of the sea. It was cool. They circled each other. Camille's being a poser and Manny's being arrogant hung in the hot air between them. They'd lock eyes and awkwardly smile before looking away again and dipping under the water. Camille thought about having lost her virginity in a jacuzzi at sixteen, before musing on the fantasies she's had over the years about mermaids and mermen, and her general tendency to get fleshy in aquatic scenarios.

Manny got cold and tried to act like he wasn't.

Then there was the sound of tiny waves lapping against the shore, and the occasional car driving past, and the laughter of their friends on the sand in the distance, and it all started speaking to them, and it said that they had been too quick to judge each other. Revealingly quick. They began to sense the knowledge that lay dormant between them. The old, quite possibly ancient, knowledge. It had been an intimidating force to encounter at first; something to inspire defensiveness. But not anymore. Now it was intoxicating. And the fact that neither of them uttered a word, and that they were both willing to honour their own thoughts, and feelings, and their constantly evolving, unspoken connection, in all of its rawness and sweetness, appealed to every heart, mind, and loin concerned.

Then there were the city lights, and the iodine smell, and the water's weightlessness, which heightened every laugh, touch, caress, and gentle, then not so gentle, kiss. Their connection was sensual, visceral, spiritual, oceanic, and, to Camille's mind, more of a one-night-thing than a Happily-Ever-After-Thing. Experiences like that are too good to be true. Experiences like that are the exception and not the rule. But, you know

life is compost

a garden

whatever

you never know what's going to grow from the seeds you plant.

Camille's looking at the countryside rolling past. It's pleasant. It isn't Europe, but it's got its own thing going on. There are fences, and paddocks, and abandoned buildings, and cows, and the occasional horse. There's a bunch of about thirty kangaroos, of all different ages, and sizes, scattered across this grassy knoll. Kangaroos freak Camille out. When she and Manny walk the dogs through different bush tracks in the evenings, clans of roos pop up out of nowhere. And, no, they don't *jump* or *leap* out of nowhere. It's their stillness that pops out of nowhere. It's their stillness that freaks Camille out.

Kangaroos-in-motion are what's expected. The silhouette of a roo side-on and on-the-go is an iconic image plastered across signs and emblems around the country, which might lead you to believe that the only encounter you're going to have with a roo will be on the road, or as they're racing across the desert at a convenient sideways angle. What you don't expect is to be faced with a kangaroo front-on, at close range, totally still, deep in the bush, where they're camouflaged against the silvery trees and the dusty earth, and you probably didn't see or sense them until now, just now, when you're a mere few feet away from at least ten of them, and they're deciding which way to move, and so are you. Yes, it is during these sudden glitches in the matrix that kangaroos become the eyes of the Australian landscape looking back at you.

Today the roos seem pretty casual, though. A couple of them are lying down, lazing about, not a care in the world. They lounge like cats. Tra-la-la. Camille is watching a joey slowly and carefully chew some grass, and she's mourning the loss of a sense of immersion that her ancestors must have had. Immersion in going one-step-at-a-time, and one-idea-at-a-time, and one-conversation-at-a-time, and one-crisis-at-a-time, and one-bite-at-a-time. All of the energy Camille spends on her phone is probably altering her DNA and the DNA of those to come after her. In fact, it *definitely* is. Like, epigenetics and everything.

Now Camille is thinking about time running out, and death, and all of those kangaroo carcasses by the road, and she wants an escape. An escape that, for better or worse, her ancestors never had.

Manny was the one that had wanted to move to the country. 'Why don't we run away together?' It was so romantic. And Camille loved the idea of becoming someone who lived outside the city with her partner. She could see herself turning into this wholesome woman who regularly attended to a sprawling vegetable and flower garden, and to a well-nourished body, and to a perfectly calm mind. But Camille now spends most of her time in regional Victoria coordinating how she's going to get to and from regional Victoria. She has yet to be changed by regional Victoria. It wants to change her. The river red gums and the yellow wattles whisper to her. 'Be still,' they say. 'Listen,' they say. 'Slow down,' they say. 'Be here,' they say. 'It's safe,' they say. 'Stop,' they say. But she refuses to listen.

Whenever Camille and Manny go for coffee in town at the place on the corner with the milk crates for seats, he reiterates how great it is to be able to walk the dogs through the bush, and how much darker the nights are, and how much brighter the stars are, and how freeing it is not to know many people and, oh! Look at the thick leaves on the apple and lemon trees! And aren't the bird sounds crazy? Is that a rosella? Then Manny will visibly sink into this feeling of relaxation and Camille will want to scream. Or to sleep. Or to run. Or to look at her phone. Or to die, maybe. Because Camille cannot sink. Camille got the job working for Holly minutes before she and Manny left the city, and now she's either at work or recovering from work.

Camille's mum, Jane, warned her that moving to regional Victoria would be challenging. But Camille could sense that underneath her mother's seemingly pragmatic concern were all of the fears that had held Jane captive throughout her life — and life is how you handle fear. So Camille convinced herself that the commute to and from the city would be easy, because heaps of people did it every day. Heaps of people handled it fine. And Camille is just like heaps of people. She could use that time on the train to become a better person. She could research some seriously meaningful shit, and listen to podcasts, and become, like, super informed. She could study perfumes, and come up with all kinds of totally genius concoctions, and devise stratagems, and become the person she's destined to be, i.e., the self-assured and super-dewy founder of a floral designing business that marries flower-essence blends and fragrances with the floral arrangements and menus of edgy, holistic, intimate events that speak to every attendee's sense of emotion and occasion

BOOM

easy

done on the train.

Meanwhile, Manny thought moving to the country would be super chill. He couldn't wait to leave the noise and the commotion of the city. He was excited to see what he and Camille would discover about themselves, and each other, when given time and space. He was excited to be at a distance from the people, routines, and places that had brought him comfort. He was keen to swap a sense of immediacy for a small town with three pubs, a train station, a handful of cabs, and a supermarket that shut at 8pm. He was excited to be obliterated and to start anew.

And when Manny began to sense that Camille was struggling to be obliterated and to start anew, he started campaigning for Camille to quit working for Holly. Because Manny is not the type of person to insist Camille keep her day job. Manny is an artist, and artists live in the abyss. Not on a salary. Not with security. An artist holds onto life itself and nothing else.

So during those long train rides when Camille wasn't sleeping or zoning out on social media, she started scrolling real estate apps trying to find a more suitable place to live. A more suitable place to live *in the city*. But she never found one, of course, because Camille and Manny's rental in the regions is bigger, better, cheaper, and more one-of-a-kind than anything within a 10, 20, 30, 40, or 50km radius of Melbourne. It's a renovated stable with a sprawling garden and an upstairs looking out over mountain tops. It has a bathtub with feet, and rooms with sunlight spilling into them at different times of the day. And, now, Camille can no longer tell the difference between what's harming her and what's helping her. Well. She can tell the difference.

She just doesn't want to.

Armadale, where Camille's work, 'Florals by Holly', is based, is on the south side of the city. And Camille is embarrassed to admit that she really likes going there every week. There's something about the veneer of wealthy suburbs that can be super comforting if you don't think about it too much or ask too many questions.

Armadale is Melbourne's Mecca for moneyed brides-to-be. There are all of these two-storey white Victorian buildings, with long chiffon curtains lining their windows, and austere signs saying things like 'by appointment only' and 'gowns by Danielle'. There are gyms, and salad bars, and nail salons, and hairdressers, and psychics. There are shops selling bronzers, and perfumes, and G-strings, and silky nighties, and ceramics, and crystals, and injectables, and strappy sandals, and açaí bowls, and spray tans. And according to what's written on Holly's inoffensive pastel-coloured website, she does floral arrangements for Melbourne's most prestigious businesses, weddings, and events. Her home page is a collage of rave reviews from various media outlets and personal endorsements from B-, C-, and D-list celebs. Holly's famous. And she's no florist. There will be no, like, 'come on in and pick your $22 bunch of dahlias.' Holly's carefully constructed buds come with a $2000 minimum spend. And Valentine's Day is D-Day. Every de rigueur hotel, brunch spot, designer boutique, and 'client-facing' company wants to set the right tone. They want their homegrown roses *peeled*. They want their face flowers, and their filler flowers, and their gesturing flowers *well organised*. They want their waratah and sweet pea *bases*. They want their brights with their brights, and their pastels with their pastels, and their bright pastels with their bright pastels, and they do *not* want their pastels with their brights.

Camille is a Dutch Masters girl when it comes to floral arranging. She likes to create treasure troves of flora where there's always more to see and know: layers, textures, shadows. She likes combining lush heirloom varietals, natives, and whatever's in season. And while she and Holly can agree on the value of something like, say, the hydrangea as a base or as a filler — and its miraculous capacity to drink from its own head — they have very different taste when it comes to flower arranging.

Holly prefers to emulate Baptiste Pitou and his prolific use of single flowers, like gypsophila, for ease of invoicing and maintenance as much as for aesthetic. Holly likes uniformity. Hierarchy. She sees rhododendrons as too suburban and the use of chemicals to dye orchids as no biggie. Holly will choose exotics over natives because she makes more money out of them. She follows what's trending. And there's no compost at Florals, because the council is just 'so hopeless' with that kind of thing, you know.

Holly opened her shop (studio? office? factory? warehouse? collective? boutique?) after ten years of working with a wedding planner based around the corner on Kooyong Road. Rumour has it he's on the verge of bankruptcy now; they never work together anymore, because said wedding planner is Holly's ex-hubby, and in order to get through the long days Camille spends with Holly, she has consciously chosen to remain largely unconscious about that. If Holly brings him up, Camille has learned to 'hmm' rather than to ask 'why?' or 'how did that happen?' or 'did you talk about that with him?' Because 'why' and 'how' and 'did you talk about it' don't exist in Holly Language. Well, they do, but they mean something different from what they mean in Camille Language.

In Camille Language, 'why' and 'how' and 'did you talk about it' are ways to further one's understanding of self and other. But in Holly Language, these kinds of questions demonstrate a lack of allegiance. They suggest that *someone* might be more inclined to ask questions, and to believe what their own eyes and ears tell them, than to believe what the Party tells them. And that's never a good look.

That's a threat.

A few years ago, Holly was looking for an assistant while in the midst of setting up her revenge-business, and Camille was working for a florist on the other side of town, but she jumped at the opportunity to work for Holly. It seemed like a huge step up in the flower world. Holly was the elegant older woman wearing denim-on-denim and stylish thick-rimmed black glasses, and looking glow-y, and perpetually tanned, and white-toothed, and naturally grey-haired in photoshoots for *Vogue Living*, because the bungalow at Sorrento was swiftly photographed pre-divorce settlement, and her English cream golden retriever, Coco, was included in the shoots, and they both came across as much more affectionate than they actually are.

Holly was the one with the epic socials and the tens-of-thousands-strong following doing floral design tutorials with popular influencers, and vloggers, and being featured in the Sunday supplements answering questions about the best way to preserve wedding bouquets. So, surely, working with her would teach Camille something. Surely, working with Holly would put Camille in contact with stylish and abundant people: people in the possession of expendable income, and expendable time, and expendable knowledge, which would save Camille from she-didn't-know-what-exactly. The only truly problematic concept was the idea of working 'with' Holly. Because Camille was never going to be working 'with' Holly. She applied for, and now has, a job working 'for' Holly.

It was humid the day Holly interviewed Camille. Wet, too. Melbourne has these uncanny tropical moments during the late spring and the early autumn. Many Indigenous Australians believe that there are up to eight seasons. But eight seasons or no, a bad hair day is a bad hair day, and Camille dreaded looking wayward during her first meeting with the ineffable Ms Hughes, because Camille is forever trying to negotiate with the inevitable. Like, if she just says *this* differently, or if she does *that* differently, or if she just wears her hair *this* way, rather than *that* way, or if she just makes a joke about *this*, or a well-timed comment about *that*, she'll avoid the inescapable.

So as Camille walked down High Street toward Florals for the very first time, taking in the homegrown designer boutiques, and the hair salons, and the smell of roasting coffee beans, she thought about her hair, and she thought about a job interview she'd had with a magazine shop years earlier in the city. She'd really wanted that job. She'd dressed in black for the interview, and she'd arrived on time with her CV, which was short, and she'd talked about her love of flowers, and gardening, and design magazines. Then the guy with the glasses in the tight shirt had said, 'you know that working here isn't glamorous, right?', and in a hundredth of a second Camille re-evaluated what she'd chosen to wear that day. She re-evaluated how she'd answered the guy's questions. She re-evaluated her posture. She re-evaluated the other women working in the store — who were quietly stacking the shelves in their three-quarter-length slacks and clogs, and looking very sad and very Melbourne — and then she re-evaluated the guy sitting in front of her who seriously believed that glamour and hard work were mutually exclusive.

Camille wove her way through Kings Arcade and arrived at Florals, a one-storey brick building near Armadale Station. It sits beside a wine bar, a barber, and a homewares shop. The front of it has a massive window with a heavy white wooden door on the left-hand side of the glass, and a light-blue neon sign in the middle of the window that says 'Florals by Holly' in a swirly font. Camille knocked on the glass, and Holly peered over her thick-rimmed black glasses from her see-through chair, behind her see-through desk, as she waved Camille in. Next to Holly was Florals' mascot, Coco, and her royal-blue velvet cushion, along with a water bowl that was empty — Camille is now the one that fills it.

Holly didn't move from her desk or get up to greet Camille when she entered the small building. She smiled without showing her teeth and observed Camille as she settled into the see-through chair opposite her own. The space smelled of dog and Chanel Coco Mademoiselle.

'Well.'

'It's sticky out there!'

'It's Camille, isn't it?'

'Yes.'

'And you have your references?'

'I have a reference, yes.'

'Just the one?'

'Yes, is that ok?'

'It's from a florist?'

'Ah, yes.'

'Have you had any experience working at a floral designing business?'

'Not technically, no.'

'Ok. Tell me about yourself, Camille.'

'Well, I've been working at Johnston Street Flowers for a few years now. They're an institution. I've learned a lot from them. But flowers and flower arranging has been a passion of mine since childhood.'

'What are your other passions?'

'I like working with flowers essences and perfumes.'

'That's very different from floral arranging.'

'I know! I guess I love anything to do with flowers.'

'What's your favourite flower?'

'Snapdragon. You?'

'Ah, difficult to say.'

'So many to choose from!'

'Yes. And what are your professional goals?'

'Right now, helping you and learning from you would be my main one.'

'Yes, but where can you see yourself in five years?'

'Here, ideally! Otherwise, I'm not sure.'

Camille lied, because she could sense Holly might not like her wanting to run her own business one day. It might make Camille seem more inclined to serve her own interests than to serve Holly's, which might make her unreliable, self-interested, and, well, a lot like Holly. So Camille's instinct was to contort herself into what she thought Holly wanted and to prioritise that over what she truly wanted for herself.

'So, what would you do in a situation where a client chooses a floral arrangement that isn't occasion appropriate?'

'Well, I would be very direct with them about the fact that they're making an unconventional choice, and I'd encourage them to either embrace that or to go with something more traditional if that's what they'd ultimately prefer.'

'And what would you do if a client wanted to use an out-of-season flower?'

'I'd always advocate for the use of seasonal flowers. But I guess if they were really keen on something, and if it was possible to get it somehow, that'd be ok? Or I'd ask you?'

'Correct.'

'Cool. Yep. *I'd ask you.*'

'What would you say are your strengths and weaknesses?'

'I'm creative and adaptable. I love collaborating. But I can get impatient, and I can doubt myself sometimes.'

'And what does the rest of your life look like?'

'Ah, I have a boyfriend.'

'What does he do?'

'He's an artist.'

'So you're the breadwinner.'

'We've never really put it in those terms?!'

'But that's the truth.'

'If the truth is that making more money than your partner makes you the breadwinner, then yes. I guess I am. At the moment.'

'You don't have to protect him. He isn't here.'

'Oh? Hah! Yeah, I know.'

'Planning to have children soon?'

'Not soon, no.'

'And you know the job on offer isn't a glamorous one?'

Camille laughed.

'Something funny?'

'No, no. I just don't find hard work and glamour to be, like, mutually exclusive.'

'Ok?'

'You seem very glamorous to me, Ms Hughes. And I also get the sense that you work very hard. So.'

'Yes, but I'm me. And you're you, Camille.'

'Right. I ... guess that's true?'

Camille had no idea what was happening, but she knew that she regretted saying anything about anything. Holly then did something on her phone, and Camille berated herself for processing her thoughts, out loud, in real time and space, *in a job interview*. Her cheeks flushed. Her heart raced. Her mouth went dry. She wasn't ready to say goodbye to the possibility of working for Holly Hughes, and to visiting Armadale each day, and to being all that she could be.

'Camille, you're unlike anyone else I've interviewed.'

'Really?'

'Yes. I want you to work for me.'

'Wow! Ok. Oh my god. Why?'

'Well, you're going to make me and my business look good. I can tell you won't get overwhelmed. Or, if you do, you won't show it. You won't bother me with it. You've had just enough experience. Not too much. You've got good taste. You're perfect.'

'Thank you, Ms Hughes. I feel honoured.'

'Call me Holly.'

'Ok! Thank you, Holly.'

Prior to the job at Florals, Camille had been working with a family business on Johnston Street in Collingwood. They insisted that she take hour-long lunch breaks. They gave her cash Christmas bonuses every year. They remembered the names of the animals that she lives with — two ex-racer greyhounds called Lola and Pope. They knew when her birthday was — April 10th, *The Day of Daring*. When they asked her how she was, they took the time to hear the answer.

They weren't interested in whether she came from wealth or where she went to school. They didn't ask leading questions about the sexual preferences of the man she lives with. They didn't jump at every opportunity to remind her of how dog-eat-dog the world is. They didn't reiterate how young and 'naive' she seems. They didn't recoil at her suggestions about how to improve different aspects of the business, because what would she know? On Valentine's Day, they closed at 5pm and had a glass of champagne with their staff before everyone headed home.

They welcomed Camille's ideas, and they welcomed her, and when she decided to leave, they were sad and excited. They made a lemon teacake and gave Camille a bouquet of jasmine, gardenia, Australian rice flowers, and peony, wrapped in magazine pages and tied with brown string, which was one of the small, economical contributions that Camille had made to the look of their business.

Then, a few months ago, Camille had run into one of the florist's daughters, Lisa, in a deli on the north side of the city. The last time Camille had seen Lisa was online, when she'd shared a picture of herself and her bearded husband holidaying in Greece and having a feast with his extended family. There was white wine, grilled fish, rocks, sea, tabbouleh.

Camille'd had too many soy caps at the deli with her sister, and upon noticing Lisa in line for the register, she stared at the oily tub of dolmades in her own hands until the clear plastic lid morphed into rainbow spots, and she wanted to weep hot, mortified tears, because Lisa represented an innocence Camille worried that she had lost.

And Lisa was probably going to ask Camille about how things were going at Florals, and Camille wouldn't know how to answer, because, on the one hand, she'd want to be honest. And, on the other hand, she'd want to lie. So, right there, holding those dolmades in that trendy deli, Camille thought that she might faint, because fainting has become a bit of a pattern, and it seems to happen when there's something or someone Camille wants to run away from.

'Camille?'

'Lisa!'

'Gosh, it's been aaaaaages.'

'I know.'

'What've you got there?'

'Dolmades. You?'

'Lewis and I are having a bit of a thing tonight, so I'm getting some antipasto.'

'Yum.'

'It's so nice to run into you!'

'You too.'

'And Florals' socials are next level, Camille. It's so cool that you work there. Seriously. Big congrats.'

'Oh? Thanks so much.'

'Ok, well, see you 'round, I guess?'

'Yeah, see you 'round, Lisa!'

Camille is thirty minutes into this train ride and she's thinking about how, over the weekend, she was concerned that her period would come today. She was relieved when she woke up this morning and didn't have it yet, because Valentine's Day. Because work. Because Holly. Because work. Because Valentine's Day. Because *sex*. Camille knows that how she relates to her body pretty much defines how she relates to everything and to everyone. Cultivating an enlivened mind-body connection is sacred. Nevertheless, she's always thankful when the needs of her body fit with her mental agenda. She's always thankful when her humanity doesn't 'get in the way' of, you know. Her 'life'.

However, ever since Camille came off the pill, a painful uterus has defined day one of her cycle, and right now, her lower back is pulsating, which is often what happens before her period comes. And the only thing worse than her period coming overnight, or sometime during this train ride, is the idea of it coming at work. You'd think that getting your period in a woman-dominated working environment would be acceptable. Or, at the very least, natural and expected. However, natural and expected events aren't highly regarded in the work environment Holly Hughes has established. Which is ironic, given it's a floral designing business, and flowers would have to be the epitome of natural and expected events. But if you were to see how Holly treats the flowers, and the clients, and the staff, and, to some extent, herself, you, too, would feel uneasy if you found yourself bleeding uncontrollably in her presence.

Camille's uterus turns into a blockade every full moon and she doesn't know whether the pain is taking her further away from what she wants or bringing her closer to it — she doesn't know what language it's speaking. Is it another sign to slow down? Or to stop? Or is it something she's supposed to push through? To fight? To override? To ignore? And why does it scramble her mental wires?

When Camille rides the Crimson Wave, it takes longer to solve problems and to respond to questions. Backhanded comments don't affect her. Over-analysing doesn't lead anywhere. On a deeper level, Camille knows that her period arriving is a resoundingly positive thing, but it doesn't meet the requirements of a 'productive' workday, or a 'productive' work environment, or the notion of 'productivity' at all. And Camille really doesn't want to be seen as unproductive or as someone who lets the team down. The prospect of not being reliable or of not making sense to others terrifies her. All of her thoughts, feelings, preferences, behaviours, and choices must be clearly labelled and understood. It's difficult for anything to operate freely in the shadows — without answers, without reasons, without names.

Camille is remembering this time she ended up in Victoria's Secret during her period. She'd gone into the city to buy a puffer jacket for the winter, and she ended up with three push-up bras, two G-strings, a bottle of kissable massage oil, a discounted watermelon lip gloss, and zero puffers. There was something about that *shop*. The pinks, the creams, the warm lighting, the heavy change-room doors, the silver handles, the smell of synthetic vanilla, the women wearing thick black eyeliner working the floor. Rather than a franchise, or a multi-billion-dollar mess, it seemed like a magical, mystical space filled with secrets. The divine feminine hijacked by something toxic, but the divine feminine no less.

Now Camille is sitting cross-legged in, like, 'ladylike' position, with one leg on top of the other, and she's crossing her arms to squeeze the ache into a smaller, more manageable morsel. But she looks defensive and tense, which she is. And being defensive and tense is quite possibly the worst thing for her, and for her uterus, and for her life. Yet Camille can't loosen up. Even if she doesn't know why she's on this train, she can't not be on this train. Even if she doesn't know why she's aching, she is. Even if she doesn't know why she forgot her phone, she did. And she wants to laugh

LAUGH

HAHAHAHAHAHAHHAHAAAAAAA

Camille is frantically hashing and rehashing what Holly might or might not ask her and what might be best to say or do. The fact it's Valentine's Day heightens the demands, the irrationality, the likelihood of making mistakes. Georgia and Alyce worked through the weekend to get everything ready for today, and Camille tried to switch off from the guilt that this induced. She used to work those days, too, but Manny encouraged her to stop.

'Your weekends are yours. And, I mean, you're essentially travelling from *interstate* every day. Georgia and Alyce have it way easier.'

'Yeah, but my "living situation" is my problem, not Holly's.'

'Yeah, but your problems become her problems. Relax so you're good for Monday.'

To make matters worse, in the midst of today's chaos, Camille is scheduled to have a meeting with her first real clients, Tim and Eric. They're getting married on the Mornington Peninsula in the spring, and they thought doing some wedding planning on Valentine's Day would be fun, so Camille booked them in. When Camille told Holly, she raised an eyebrow, but she didn't protest. She just kept editing Florals' social media post of the wisteria arch that Camille, Georgia, and Alyce had assembled for the influencer wedding in St Kilda last week — without tagging or thanking any of them for their input.

Tim works in fashion and Eric is a gallery owner. Or he might be a curator. The two of them explain themselves so fast and with such vigour that Camille often loses what they're saying altogether. And Eric is a pale peroxide-blond porcelain doll. He wears tightly fitted blazers in a way that makes Camille think it must be his 'thing'. She could imagine Eric owning a whole assortment of fitted blazers in different colours, and from different designers and tailors, and that people probably remember him by his blazers. Like, 'oh, the blazer guy?' And 'hey, love the brocade!' And 'super Chuck Bass!' And 'so friggin' suave!'

Tim is very into eye contact. It's as if he's making an assessment of the health of Camille's insides through her eyeballs while she's speaking, and at their last meeting she wondered if he might be able to see the anger in her liver, which her Chinese Medicine doctor had told her about, and she came to the conclusion that he probably could. Tim is brown-skinned and brown-eyed, and even in a relatively loose pair of cream trousers and a shirt, it's obvious that he's sculpted like Discobolus.

The first time Camille met Tim and Eric at Florals, she

didn't know what to say to them. Whenever she spoke, she became hyper aware of the sounds coming out of her mouth, and of her cheeks flushing, and of the fact that she existed, and that she was being seen and heard. Then she'd started asking redundant questions, and trying to think of funny things to say, and nodding, and 'hmmhmmming' a lot.

The second time they met up, Camille decided to do something different, because if you want something to *be* different, you have to *do* something different. So she stopped trying to keep up. She stopped trying to whip out the one-liners. She listened. And while Tim and Eric were busy discussing Eric's mother's disdain for soy and soy-based candles, and laughing about Tim's gargantuan family coordinating cheap flights to Australia and rental cars to the coast, Camille saw pale pinks and pistachios. A sea of blush and *Epacris impressa* reaching across exposed brick, timber cladding, and old machinery. She could smell metal and daphne. She could taste rosé. She could touch thick glass baubles, soft cloth napkins, grapevines. She could hear 'I Want You' by Savage Garden. She began to sense that she was the continuation of something, and that it was about joining with it, not forcing it.

Camille is stressing about how Georgia and Alyce will have been at Florals for hours before she gets there today, because Holly will definitely find a way to use this — and the fact that Camille has scheduled a meeting with Tim and Eric — against her at some point. She'll be like, 'oh, how nice of you to show up, would you mind staying back *for no extra pay?*' or 'oh, so glad you decided to make an appearance, could you *scrub the warehouse floor for the next three days?*' Camille's body just produced a rush of 'device, now, please' and she couldn't answer its call.

She couldn't run.

Camille ran daily when she was in high school: around the block, around the Botanical Gardens, around the school oval, any oval. She and Manny ran from the city. She dreams of running from Holly. She wants to run from this phone-less moment with herself. But she hasn't actually run in years. Time, money, plans, people.

Camille is twisting in her seat and looking out the window again. She really wants to be someone who is so immersed in what she's doing that her phone is this, like, pesky afterthought. You know. It's an *annoyance*. Whenever she's meeting up with friends, she makes sure not to have it on her. It can be in her bag or in her pocket. It just can't be in her hands or readily visible on her person in any way. Then she'll check it in the bathroom or when she gets back to the car. Like, in secret.

Because Camille wants her inboxes, and her message banks, and her DMs, to be overflowing with offers and opportunities, and with people desperately wanting her attention, and inviting her to things, and complimenting her on stuff. So every 'check' becomes a prayer. A supplication for feeling as if she's of value, because her time is in high demand. Her time is *precious*. And without others wanting her time, Camille fears that her time means nothing.

She's tried turning her notifications off. She's tried putting her phone on flight mode, but she always switches it back on shortly thereafter to 'look something up' or to 'check the weather' or to 'see her bank balance', because her bank isn't a bank, it's an app, and the current temperature isn't outside, it's on her phone.

Camille knows that having the internet at her fingertips hasn't made her a better or more intelligent person, because having knowledge is very different from being knowledgeable. But what if something goes wrong? What if she gets lost? What if there's an emergency? What if she doesn't read a message, or see a missed call, or receive an update, or read a pertinent piece of news, or transfer another hundred bucks from her savings account? Manny never has his wallet on him. No one can be relied upon. Camille is alone in the universe and *she is not to be blamed for the state of herself!*

Camille goes to her phone looking for relief and comes away from it feeling remorse. A remorse she can't really explain because, technically, she isn't doing anything wrong by checking it. Technically, she's just doing what everyone else is doing. But then she'll look at the clouds beyond the bedroom window, and at the flowers in the garden, and at the dogs, and at Manny, and a feeling of guilt will expand into every cell of her being, as if she's missing out on her own life, and she'll want to fall to her knees and check her phone again.

Manny lasted a year on social media before bailing. He loved chat rooms as a teenager because he could message girls from school and send them poems. Then he thought he needed social media for his writing, so he'd create imagery to accompany bits of his work, before he realised that he wanted his poetry to be published. He wanted his poetry to be in journals. He wanted people to be able to hold his poetry in their hands.

And spending hours curating an online profile led to a sense of hopelessness that would strip Manny of the desire to write altogether. He'd start telling himself scary stories about how everything has been said before, and AI is taking over everything, anyway, so what difference does it make? What difference does *he* make?

Manny is also an aesthete, and he's always had problems with the look of social media. Bright. Blocky. Sterile. Authoritarian. And this disdain has given him a bit of an edge, and a healthy sense of superiority in relation to technology, which, occasionally, has enabled him to keep writing. To keep thinking. To keep reminding himself that he exists. To keep reminding the universe that it exists.

So, on a particularly despondent Wednesday, he might get into the bath at 3pm with the intention of 'unwinding' and, before he knows it, he'll be writing with a ferocity and a conviction he didn't know he possessed, and when a particularly good line strikes him, and moves him, he'll feel hope again. Then he'll start telling himself happy stories about how AI can never take everything over, because there are so many things it can never know. There are so many things it can never predict, write, calculate, copy, buy, or plan. There are so many things that have a heart.

Still, there's always the possibility that, one day, Manny's writing will be cancelled by actual people. He'll be labelled an _____, thanks to some one-liner he wrote a decade ago that's been taken out of context. Unflattering photos from his online profile(s) will resurface, and he'll look untrustworthy and sweaty, and his voice will shake as falsely earnest newsreaders with ear pieces and two minutes counting down ask him seemingly simple questions that are actually complex philosophical dilemmas, and then Camille will leave him, and he'll drink too much whiskey, and his liver will suffer, and he'll hang himself, and in fifty or one hundred years his work will be cherished and longed for, because it came from simpler, more poetic times.

Camille wishes that screaming and crying in public was an ok thing. Maybe there wouldn't be wars if everyone was used to screaming and crying happening at random — on trains, in offices, at bars, outside shops, while seated at cafes, in post office queues. There'd be no need for violence or for trying to control others. Everyone could scream or cry for a sec and move on. Nothing personal. No biggie. Just the usual, mate. You know how it is.

Although, there are certain public situations in which screaming and crying are not only accepted but encouraged — and thank god for them. Last autumn, Camille and Manny drove into the city to watch the Australian Football League's ANZAC Day Eve game. Everyone living in or around Melbourne has an AFL team. It doesn't matter if they claim to have 'never watched' the AFL or if they insist that they 'hardly follow it' or if they're really 'not that into' it. If they were born in Melbourne, their family has a team and, by association, they have a team. If they aren't from Melbourne, but they married someone from Melbourne, they have a team. If they moved from overseas, or from interstate, and they've lived in Melbourne, they have a team. And, conveniently, Manny and Camille both barrack for the Dees, aka the Melbourne Demons.

Camille feels bad she's not as interested in the women's football league. She's glad it exists, and if she'd been able to play AFL when she was at school, she absolutely would've. It's just hard to beat the primal interest she has in watching oiled-up fit young dudes run around in tighty-whities. And, clearly, Camille isn't alone in thinking or feeling this way, because she and Manny were just two bodies among a hundred thousand shuffling through the Melbourne Cricket Ground's gates before the game, and filling the stadium, ready to shout, ready to cry, ready to clap, ready to cheer.

Camille once watched a French-Canadian film in which a character commented that the Abenaki Native American Indians believe that there are five ways to heal: laughing, crying, talking, moving your body, and screaming. And Camille could see all of these at work among those in attendance at the MCG that night.

Before half-time, Camille wove her way through the cement corridors and stairwells to get more snacks and beers for her and Manny, and when she finally got to the nearest food-and-drink stall, the staff were totally focused on the game. The security guards, the baristas, the cleaners, the cops, the bartenders, the ushers. It was hard to get anyone's attention to pay for her $5 chips, because sportsmen aren't just sportsmen. They're shamans. They take on the pain and passion of an entire community. They're symbols of triumph and tragedy. They're scapegoats.

And because it was ANZAC Day Eve, before the match, the memorial flame was lit, and everyone in the crowd held up their phones like candles. The Australian and New Zealand national anthems were sung by a woman who used to be on *Neighbours*, and the war medals glistened under the lights, and the minute of silence was had, and the soldier's trumpet cried out, and as Camille sipped her Victoria Bitter, it occurred to her that society has so many costumes, and rituals, and sacrifices. It has so many hierarchies, and expectations, and codes of conduct. Society is a cult.

Then a bunch of players started brawling near the boundary line during the third quarter. Sledging, shoving. Ripping shirts. The crowd kept eating snacks, and beaming and hollering, and trying to film the scuffle on their phones, and Camille started thinking about what would happen if the crowd became violent. Shamans hold a lot of power. If the right one says the wrong thing at the right time, what was once unified could quickly divide. Lest we forget. Or, as Manny whispered under his breath to Camille after the minute of silence, 'lesty, lesty, forgetty, forgetty.'

There's this older guy sitting across the aisle from Camille. He must be in his sixties. He got on the train after she did. He's wearing a flannel shirt and jeans. His hands are in his lap and he's looking out the window. The skin on his face is dry and tanned, and full of deep, uncompromising crevices. He doesn't have a phone, or a newspaper, or a book, or a pair of headphones. There's dirt under his fingernails. He must be a farmer or something. And every time Camille has looked at him, he's been looking out the window. Like, *engrossed*. A few times she's stared at him for a bit too long to see if he could sense her staring at him, and he couldn't. Or, at least, he acted like he couldn't.

Camille is wondering why he's travelling into the city today. Maybe he's visiting a family member in the hospital. Or maybe he has a meeting with a lawyer. Or maybe he's going shopping for appliances. Or maybe he has a Valentine in the city and they're going to make a day of it. Or maybe he's going to talk to someone about his phone plan. Camille is bored. Her brain bores her. It just keeps jibber-jabbering on. She's never going to know what he's up to, so who cares? Why is she even *THINKING* about it? What's the *POINT*? Surely there are more important things to be *CONTEMPLATING* and *REFLECTING* upon. Like, when is she finally going to have all of those *BIG THOUGHTS* that *SOLVE ALL OF HER PROBLEMS*?

It's so weird how the most genius and influential people on the planet have looked at the same sky, and walked on the same soil, and breathed the same air as Camille. They've been in the same world when they've thought the thoughts, and felt the feelings, that have led them to greatness. They've dealt with bosses, and with money, and with parents, and with lovers, and with technology, and with bodies, and with co-workers, and with governments, and with pain, and with random people on their chosen mode of transport. They've questioned who and what their silences have belonged to. They've been a part of the greater mind of which Camille is a part. She's at one with them, and with all that came before her, and with everything that is to come after.

Camille has never been able to work on the train. She's looked at fellow commuters highlighting, and speed-reading, and filling in crazy-looking graphs, and she's felt sick. It's as if there's not a moment to spare, not a moment to lose, to rest, to imagine. It's as if a person's only value is in what they do, rather than in what they are.

Camille usually listens to healing hertz frequencies or atmospheric tracks with titles like 'Forever' and 'Hypnotise' as she gazes out the window and thinks about where she and Manny want to buy property one day. Maybe an hour from Byron Bay. Not too far from the beach. Somewhere enveloped by thick green tropical leaves. Moist soil. White sand. Seaweed. Possibility. Fecundity. Frangipani.

At bedtime, Camille flips through books on Mediterranean interior design before she falls asleep. Her dreams absorb the marés walls, and the arched doorways, and the olive trees, and the terracotta tiles, and the pinewood tables. She inhales a bit deeper. She's reminded that she's alive, and that anything is possible, before Holly flashes across her mind, and Camille chastises herself for being lofty and impatient — failing to recognise that patience is different from subservience. And that dreaming precedes reality.

About a year ago, Camille made the mistake of sharing her tropical Mediterranean-Australian dream with Holly. 'That's why I hired *you*, you know,' Holly hath protested. 'So that *I* could spend more time at the bloody beach.' Holly doesn't give a fuck about the beach. She sold her half of the Sorrento bungalow in a heartbeat. She clings to the city like a junkie, and she gets frustrated when the Christmas/ New Year break rolls around, because she hates the way everything slows down for a couple of weeks. Argh. Keep going, everybody. Never stop. Don't stop. Slow down and die. *Slow down and die.*

Camille gets the sense Holly doesn't have much family or many friends. An estranged daughter was mentioned in passing once, and Camille could sense Holly's regret for having let this information slip, so Camille has never brought it up again. There are a few girlfriends around Melbourne from 'back in the day', but, overall, an almost psychotic loneliness seems to run Holly's life. So, to Holly, being at the beach means being alone. She's really only interested in 'the joys of nature' when high-status clients say that they are. However, this didn't stop her from telling Camille all about how expensive and horrific Byron Bay is these days — as if everybody doesn't know that. And because Holly's listening skills are largely non-existent the whole 'maybe an hour away from Byron Bay' thing got a bit lost in translation. But Holly's antics haven't deterred Camille. Because even if Camille doesn't know exactly what somewhere maybe an hour away from Byron Bay has to offer, there's definitely something.

And it calls to her when she listens to music on the train.

When Camille was a kid, she became obsessed with King Arthur and the Knights of the Round Table. She had the novels and the picture books. She watched the films. And while most kids become fixated on particular characters — there are plenty to choose from between Lancelot, Merlyn, Guinevere, The Lady of the Lake, King Arthur, Morgan le Fay — Camille fell in love with Avalon. She would fantasise about it to get through the day at school, and to survive long car trips, and to fall asleep on hot nights. She would imagine its waters. Its mountains. Its flowers. Its mist. Every day, she would travel to the place that created Excalibur.

The place you can't find unless you believe that it's there.

Camille and Manny went to a Kurt Vile gig last winter when he and his band somehow made their way to regional Victoria, and all of the cool kids in town went, in their woollen coats and worn caps.

Before the concert, Manny and Camille lit candles, and sat with the dogs, and smoked biodynamic weed from a golden pipe, and drank negronis, and ate veggie crisps, and with each sip, puff, pat, and nibble, Camille knew the physical world to be spiritual. She could feel it humming, like when she works with flowers and stumbles upon an arrangement that moves her; like when she tastes the tiny strawberries she and Manny have managed to grow in the garden during the summer; like when she distils rose essence using her grandmother's old distiller, and the kitchen, house, and road down to the golf course at the end of the street become charged by the flower's defiant aroma. It is in these moments that Camille knows her life is a temple. The only question is how she's going to show her devotion.

Then Camille and Manny half-walked and half-ran into town in the dark. They laughed about missing the whole thing because they were high, and they'd chosen to travel on foot to save money, and wasn't life ridiculous. They saw an owl. And a rabbit. After a period of silence, Manny asked Camille how she was doing, and she said, 'good, yeah ... Just, ah, *being Camille*.'

They made it to the old theatre, and they got more negronis, and Kurt played 'Palace of OKV in Reverse' for what felt like hours. It made Camille think about how something that can change a person's mood, and unite people across race, gender, age, language, neurology, religion, and socio-economic status, has to be the most powerful force in the universe. She could feel her body and all of the other bodies

in one hundred years
gone
but
right now
a symphony of vibration
yes
the feeling is real
in fact
maybe
the feeling
is the only thing that is.

Camille has drifted off. She's walking down a path, which she doesn't recognise. She's tripped and sunk deeper into her seat on the train. She's adjusted her head against the window, and she's carrying on down the path, and arriving at an orchard.

Rows and rows of orange and apple trees, all in bloom. She's stopping to smell them. They're pungent and sweet. She's remembering that orange-blossom essence helps to cultivate peace and relaxation and apple blossom is for clarity. Camille would love to bottle them up, but she can hear some sort of event happening in a nearby clearing. Laughter and music. The vibration of celebration. She's getting closer to it, and she's wondering if Manny's there. Is that where they decided to meet? Or was she meant to go somewhere else?

There are long timber tables with candelabras and orange and apple blossoms bursting from vases. There are blossoms scattered along the ground and in people's hair. Everyone is dressed in coloured togas. Camille is in a toga, too. It's violet.

Her least favourite colour. Oh, well. And where's Manny? He must be here somewhere.

Everybody's smiling, and telling Camille to grab a plate, and to get a drink. She knows no one, but they seem to know her, so she's going along with it. She doesn't want to be rude, or to miss the opportunity to be appreciated, and accepted, and to maybe have a good time. She's trying to find her seat, and everybody's spot is labelled, but she can't find hers. That can't be right. Everyone seems to know her. She's definitely supposed to be here.

There are small brown vials at the centre of each place setting, and they're covered in pictures of orange and apple blossoms. She picks one up and opens it. The scent turns her body into the orchard. This is her event. This is her creation. Oh, no. There's blood on her toga —

'Darl, your ticket?'

'Oh!'

'Sorry to wake you!?'

'It's ok. Here.'

Please don't ask to see a concession card
Please don't ask to see a concession card

'Thanks, love. Have a good one. *Sleep well.*'

'Ha, thanks!'

The other night, Manny asked Camille why she's still working at Florals, and she got really angry, because she has no idea. Although, instead of admitting this, she gave a melodramatic and drawn-out speech about how sorry she is that she's not content doing odd jobs around the house all day like he is. Sorry she wants things. Sorry she's working toward things. Things that she feels very strongly about, even if she doesn't know exactly what they are, and for some reason they make her more susceptible to the whims of an embittered older woman who is thriving off an assortment of assets, a series of divorce settlements, trust funds, and carefully orchestrated interest payments. Yet she's always late to pay Camille. Oh, yes. Holly couldn't *bear* to be paid late herself. Not for a minute. But she doesn't see the hypocrisy of putting Camille in that situation. But at least Camille's *TRYING*. At least she's *PUTTING HERSELF OUT THERE*.

Then Manny quoted a line from *Star Wars* and Camille

stormed out of the room, before she returned a few minutes later and rested her head in his lap like a bitch.

Camille can't explain her lack of faith in herself. She's lived a safe and happy life. Her parents are still alive and in love, so they say. She went to a private school before going to Melbourne Uni. She didn't finish uni, because fuck that shit. But she went. She had the *opportunity* to go. And when Camille talks to her sister, Clarice, the tension that simmers between them is pretty textbook. Manny's family is way more messed up. So Camille doesn't know why dread festers at her core so intensely. Or why she feels stuck so much of the time. And when she looks at Manny looking at her as if she's stuck, she feels triple the sense of fear and helplessness, because she has no clue what to do about it, and it's hard enough to admit this to herself, let alone to him.

Then Camille doubles down, and she justifies the fear-based decisions she's making, because *OF COURSE* she's staying in a job that makes her miserable, and *OF COURSE* she's on social media comparing herself to others and feeling like crap, and *OF COURSE* she's overly reliant on stimulants, and *OF COURSE* she's putting up with things she shouldn't, because 'that's what you do' and 'that's life'. But that's not life. That's death.

And, deep down, Camille knows it.

Manny fears being seen as poor more than he fears poverty itself. He feels no shame about living on welfare and the occasional thousand pounds from his British dad. Yet whenever Manny goes out, which isn't often, he spends more time in front of the mirror getting ready, and analysing how others might see him, than anyone else Camille has met, dated, befriended, or lived with.

And, as a result of Manny's wardrobe dysphoria, he's spent years scouring regional thrift shops for the most well-worn cottons, and the most perfectly cut jeans, and the most cumbersome leather belts. One time, he went to a tailor in the town where they live, and the woman noticed the designer labels in Manny's trousers and charged him double what she had charged Camille to take up her jeans a few weeks prior, not knowing that the pants had cost Manny $5, and that he was basically a pauper. Just a very well-dressed one.

Manny plays his guitar some days, and RuneScape other

days, before he writes something down, has a bath, worries about making *actual* money, and goes out into the garden with the dogs. Lola and Pope cost eighty bucks each. They were bred together, they trained together, they raced together, and they were held in captivity together. Pope is black and ripped with spots of white. Lola is skinny, veiny, and caramel coloured. Lola is scared of flies, and Pope starts shaking whenever a ute with a rattling tray drives past. The two of them lie about on bulbous cushions all day and then they do 'zoomies', sprinting around Manny and Camille in circles when they take them for a walk. But they never run away. Even if they were born to run, they're very loyal, as traumatised creatures often are.

Manny and Camille adopted the dogs when Manny had a book of poems called *TAKE THIS EXIT* published. He hasn't written anything since. He says that the next book's 'coming' and that there's 'no rush', but Camille thinks he's scared of writing another one, because the process of writing the first one was so gruelling. Manny had to face himself every day. Then he'd get finicky with Camille about how she peeled the potatoes, and how she hung their woollen jumpers on the washing line, before he'd launch into rants about his dad, and about his mates, and about different rugby coaches, and football players, and cricket captains. 'All of these broken fucking men. What the *FUCK*. They're so *IRRESPONSIBLE*. They've made themselves *REDUNDANT*. All they do is *TAKE* and *SHUFFLE ABOUT* being *OVERWEIGHT* and *PRETENDING* that they *STAND* for something. Acting as if they can *THINK* for themselves.'

Sometimes Manny wonders if he's destined to become an art critic, or an English teacher, or an ad man. Maybe poetry is just a rite of passage, kind of like how acting is for heaps of people. Because, like, wtf, dude? Thirty's a'knocking and how many hours have you spent 'bank standing' and trying to get '99 Magic'?

It didn't help that one of Manny's mates from university, Flynn, had his novella published a year ago and was immediately lauded as The Voice of a Generation. Flynn is Aboriginal and the book was critically acclaimed as 'groundbreaking'. But, jealousy aside, it was what Manny learned when he finally had a craft beer with Flynn at the local pub while Flynn was touring the regions to promote his magnum opus that depressed him the most.

Flynn was smoking rollies, and picking at the dry skin around his fingernails, and adjusting his beanie at different intervals as he told Manny he was on welfare, too. His novella had been acquired by a conglomerate, and it was being translated into seven different languages. A production company was eyeing the film rights, and the book was, according to every newspaper, 'The New Australian Odyssey'. Yet Flynn was still living in squalor. 'It's pretty funny,' he grinned. 'Or, at least, it's ironic, given that the only way anyone makes money in the publishing or film industries is if people pay for what writers write.'

Manny asked Flynn why he didn't demand more money, and Flynn said that it hadn't occurred to him. If people didn't see the value in his being paid more, then that was that. Manny banged his head on the table, and Flynn put his arm around his shoulders. 'You've gotta pick your battles, mate,' he laughed. 'You've gotta pick your battles.'

Sometimes, when Camille is struggling with her own life and she gets tired of thinking about Manny's life, she starts worrying about Clarice's life.

Camille is embarrassed that both her and her sister's names start with a 'C'. She's never had the gall to ask their parents why they decided to do that because, regardless, their answer is going to suck. It's either going to be 'because we liked the sound of it' or 'we actually didn't think about it' or 'we thought you'd start an ethical fashion brand together and/ or be failed folk singers'.

Apparently, Jane kind-of-sort-of named Clarice after Clarice Beckett, which Camille believes to be the equivalent of cursing her. To Camille, Clarice Beckett's life, and art, is some of the most depressing shit this nation has ever produced. And, like a self-fulfilling prophecy, Clarice lives a lonely and depressing life. But she'll be the last to admit it, which is always the sign of someone living a *truly* lonely and depressing life, not simply an *existentially* lonely and depressing life. Like, an *actually* lonely and depressing life.

Clarice is older than Camille by three years. They have similar colouring, but Clarice seems paler. They've got similar builds, but Clarice seems smaller. Clarice has been studying philosophy for the last decade. She loves academia and academia loves her. Her PhD is on something to do with the environment, which she doesn't give a fuck about, and Camille knows this because Clarice told her one time. Not in those words, but basically. Nevertheless, friends and family see Clarice as an angel. She's so 'sweet' and 'humble' and 'unassuming'. They see Camille as difficult by comparison, because she has a habit of wanting things and of being indignant about things. So they assume that Camille can take care of herself. And they might be right.

But, because people have deemed Camille to be more headstrong and capable than she feels herself to be, and because people have deemed Clarice to be calmer and sweeter than she knows herself to be, over time, an awkward distance developed between the two young women.

It didn't help that Camille idolised Clarice when they were younger. There's something about idolising a person that can alienate them from you. But Clarice was just *so cool*. So fragile and rebellious. So Kat from *10 Things I Hate About You*. She would sit in iconic cafes on Brunswick Street like Mario's, and order long blacks, and read weighty European literature: Dostoyevsky, Proust, Tolstoy. She'd wear turtlenecks and plaid pants. She'd hang out with older guys and argue over 'isms'. Camille absolutely wanted to be her.

Then something happened. Camille still isn't sure what. But Clarice went on medication to manage her moods, and her eyes emptied. She became distracted and docile.

71

Camille was furious at Clarice's doctor, or psychiatrist, or whoever it was that prescribed the pills she was on, because they clearly weren't helping, and nothing was done about it. Everyone was so busy feeling relieved that 'sweet' Clarice was 'getting help' that no one recognised there might be a problem. Then Clarice started seeing a new doctor, because her usual one went on maternity leave, and she was put on a new drug, in addition to what she was already on, and she became vulnerable in a way that frightened Camille.

Now Camille is replaying phone conversations she and Clarice had during that time in her mind, because she's still searching for answers.

'So how is everything?'

'Good, yeah. I'm just tired.'

'You're always tired.'

'Am I?'

'Yes.'

'Isn't everyone tired?'

'I don't know.'

'How's Florals?'

'The same. Holly still hasn't given me a raise. Or proper clients.'

'Still?'

'Still.'

'That sucks.'

'Yep.'

'What're you going to do?'

'I don't know. How's your new doctor?'

'She's ok. Kind of formal.'

'But how's your, like, mood?'

'What do you mean?'

'You seem flat.'

'I'm always flat.'

'Flatter than usual.'

'And what would you know about it?'

'Nothing?'

'Mmm.'

'So do you want to talk to me about it?'

'There's nothing to talk about.'

'Ok.'

'And maybe I don't *want* to talk about it.'

'Ok, but how is anyone supposed to help you if you don't want to talk about it?'

'I don't need help, Camille.'

'Right.'

'Seriously.'

'What?'

'Just let it go.'

'Ok, ok.'

When Camille had the job at the florist on Johnston Street, she used to sell lilies to this guy every Wednesday at two o'clock. He'd walk in with his long grey hair, which he wore in a low ponytail. He'd be in a short-sleeved shirt, no matter what the temperature was. He had a tattoo of an anchor running along the inside of his forearm. He smelled like tobacco.

One Wednesday, Camille plucked up the courage to ask him about who he was and what he did. He told her that he'd worked the suicide line for years and that a friend from that time wasn't doing too well. She was old and she lived nearby. Camille asked him about what he said to people back then. How he helped them without … helping. He took a deep breath and looked down at the lilies in his hands.

'Suicide is a funny thing.'

'Yeah.'

'What the person wants is to die, right? But not really. Not when it comes down to it. When it comes down to it, they want a fresh start. They want something hard that they're going through to be over and for something new to begin. They just can't see how else to go about it.'

'So how do you help them? To see how else to go about it?'

'You can't, doll. You can't help them to see anything. You've just gotta be there. Whether they stay or whether they go on ahead.'

When Clarice attempted suicide, no one but Camille knew it was coming. And there's no triumph in that. Being the one who knew is a burden. Camille still wishes she'd been wrong and that everyone else had been right. Then, she would've just been overreacting and paranoid — and she'd rather live with that than with the truth. Because the truth is that Clarice called 000 after ingesting a bunch of pills and lying down to die. She'd written letters to everyone. She'd organised for her landlord to check the air conditioner the next morning so that he'd be the one to find her. But something overcame Clarice as her vision blurred — and it said to call for help. Then she ended up in hospital for weeks. Camille visited her multiple times. And, in some unfortunate yet miraculous way, it brought them closer together.

'Hey.'

'Hi.'

'Sorry I couldn't get here until now.'

'It's ok.'

'No, it isn't.'

'Ok?'

'Sorry. I'm overwhelmed. I got you some flowers. They're natives. And here's a honey perfume and a bush flower essence. The flower essence is a blend of, ah. Tall yellow top and waratah.'

'What does it do?'

'You take a few drops of it under the tongue a couple of times a day. It's gentle. Flower essences are basically water. Energetically imprinted water. There's nothing left of the actual flower or anything that could interfere with whatever they've got you on.'

'Yeah, but what does it do?'

'Well, tall yellow top is supposed to help shift feelings of isolation. Waratah is good for rebuilding strength and stuff. Honey is super comforting and it's meant to, like, help you to connect with the sweetness of life.'

'Thank you.'

'Has no one else brought you flowers?'

'No. Maybe people don't have much sympathy for *the mentally ill.*'

'You're not mentally ill, Clarice.'

'Yes, I am.'

'No, you're not.'

'What am I then?'

'You're sad. You're depressed. You're anxious. You're not crazy, you're human.'

'That's not what the doctors are saying.'

'Why are you listening to what the doctors are saying?'

'They know what they're talking about.'

'You know you better than anyone else, Clarice. Only you are inside you.'

'Sometimes it doesn't feel that way.'

Camille couldn't remember the last time she'd seen her sister cry. It must've been when they were watching *The Notebook*. Clarice turned away and Camille sat down on the bed and rested her hand on her sister's.

'It's ok.'

'God. Sorry. I haven't cried in such a long time. And no one has touched me since I got here except for the nurse who put the drip in. It's like everyone is ... scared.'

'Yeah, well, you scared everyone.'

'Camille?'

'Yeah?'

'Could you hug me?'

'Of course.'

'It's just that sometimes it feels like I'm supposed to survive without hugs or without asking for hugs. And I don't know how to, you know. Ask.'

'Why didn't you call me?'

'I don't know. The same reason I haven't asked for hugs when I needed to, probably.'

There's this half-built abandoned temple on the way into the city outside Footscray. It has a massive sixteen-metre cream-coloured statue of the Heavenly Queen Goddess of the Sea (Mazu) 天后媽祖簡介 presiding over it, and there's graffiti on its crumbling walls, and scaffolding circling it. It's right on the Maribyrnong River and today there are a couple of people cycling past. Camille dreamed about it once. She often dreams of water. Of tsunamis. Of skyscrapers being swallowed up by rivers. Of cliffs adjacent to roaring seas. But deep water terrifies Camille the most. Basically any body of water that she can't touch the ground in. And all of the times that she's swam beyond where she could feasibly stand haunt her. Being suspended like that.

Wtf.

Camille wishes that she had packed some of her flower essences along with her night-blooming-jasmine perfume. She recently made an essence from pomegranate flower and red hibiscus, which is perfect for when she's feeling trapped in her body and angsty like this.

A psychic at South Melbourne Market told Camille that she was a monk in a past life. The woman could see an Italian monastery in the sixteenth century. An apothecary. Perfumes, unguents, poisons, flames. Camille laughed in a way that could almost be described as fearful, but it was probably closer to a kind of recognition, and relief.

However, Camille has become too nervous to bring flower essences into work. At first, she hadn't considered what might happen if Holly saw them, and this was her first misstep. Holly watches what Camille ingests like a hawk. Then she talks about how she wishes she still had her younger body, and how she envies Camille's, and, no, she can't eat plant-based, because her bones are brittle and she needs calcium, but kale won't do. Imagine how much kale she'd need to get the adequate amount of calcium. *Cow's milk and only cow's milk, Camille.*

So when Holly caught Camille casually dropping some banksia under her tongue at her desk one day it was

GAME

ON

She launched into another hours-long, semi-Shakespearan reflection upon her epic twenty-something self, and how she, too, used to make flower essences, and how she, too, knows *all* about them. Implying that Camille knows nothing about them, and that she's effectively stealing the act of making flower essences from Holly herself, because Holly understands more about them than Camille ever could, even though Camille has never seen Holly *TAKING* flower essences nor *MAKING* them nor *DISCUSSING* them nor *RESEARCHING* them nor *MENTIONING* them in *ANY FORM* or in *ANY WAY* until *NOW*

JUST NOW

And never mind that flower essences have been around for hundreds, thousands, and possibly millions of years, and when you stop and think about how many generations of people this knowledge has passed down through, and how many individuals have spent time and energy dedicating themselves to the building up and passing on of this knowledge across different cultures and continents, it's astonishing.

But, according to Holly, Camille needn't bother with flower essences, because she knows nothing about them, really, and she'd have to do a course. Multiple courses, in fact. Flowers and their essences are very complex. Very big and scary. And maybe the flowers don't want to be talked about so much anymore, anyway? Maybe they don't want to continue being utilised, celebrated, and studied? Maybe the flowers want to be left *ALONE*

Camille couldn't tell if Holly was making such a big deal about it because she wanted to start making flower essences again herself, or because she wanted to share more about her life with Camille, or because she wanted to undermine Camille's confidence so that, one fateful day when someone who runs a successful flower-essence business walks into Florals, Holly will be all like, 'oh, Camille makes flower essences, don't you, hun? You two should *talk.*' And Holly will say this knowing that speaking to the Uber-Successful Flower Essence Business Person will either embolden Camille, or it will make her feel inadequate, and Holly will be more than happy to take a gamble on the latter, because she knows that the flower essences Camille makes are on a completely different scale. They're on a windowsill-scale. A hobbyist-scale. And you just can't have it all, you know? Holly's learned *that* the hard way. And she just wants to help Camille, really. It's for her own good in the end. You never know, though.

Maybe Camille would end up working for the Uber-Successful Flower Essence Business Person. Maybe they would treat her with kindness, and respect, and Camille would flourish, because that's all people need to flourish. Kindness and respect. Dread and doubt may be universal, but so is what helps people. So is what makes life worth living. So maybe Camille would find herself mastering what she's passionate about, and she'd contribute it to the flower world, and to the business world, and to the actual world, and she'd wear so much linen, and her skin wouldn't get dry in the winter anymore. It'd be so, so dewy.

Then maybe Camille would turn into someone who

could *TRUST* life and she'd bleed *FREELY* and she'd live on a *HUGE PROPERTY* with the *DOGS* and with *MANNY* like total *UNDER THE TUSCAN SUN VIBES* and the two of them would build *WALLS* together from *STONE* and make *LOVE* on *HIGH-THREAD-COUNT SHEETS* and have *SPECIAL BABIES* unlike *OTHER PEOPLE'S BABIES* and time would become *ELASTIC* and there would be *ENDLESS FLOWERBEDS* and *VEGETABLE PATCHES* and *HERB GARDENS* and *JOY* growing *EVERYWHERE* and Camille would be like, wow, Holly. Thank you. All of this

is because of you.

Southern Cross Station is chaos this morning. It's raining, so the streets beyond the building's walls are splashing and heaving with dirty water, which always makes everything seem louder and more hectic inside the station. Well, Southern Cross is always loud and hectic. Camille is just more attuned to it today, because she doesn't have any vaporwave to give it a rosy glow. She's more aware than ever of the fact that everyone around her has tiny little umbrellas to protect themselves from the elements, and tiny little devices plugged into their tiny little skulls, because *aren't we the robots we fucking fear*! *Eyes Wide Fucking Shut*! Cheers to *fuckin' that*! Happy fuckin' *Valentine's Day*!

A few years ago, when Camille saw a Chinese Medicine doctor about regulating her hormonal cycle, he told her that a woman's body is governed by many different systems and organs, and that for Camille, her liver was the most sensitive part of the equation — and the liver is associated with anger.

So when Camille is at home, and period pain starts, she'll beat the bed or go for a walk. But Camille's got nowhere to go right now. The bathrooms are in the opposite direction, so she can't hide out in a cubicle for a minute, and clench her fists, and silent-scream. She's considering going into the newsagents and crying into a random magazine during the seven minutes that she has to get to Platform 10, but no. She isn't going to do that, either. She's going to the platform. Come on, legs. Come on, feet.

Sometimes Camille feels like having a body is like having a pet. Or a prisoner. It's, like, why won't you do what you're told to do? When you're told to do it? It's been explained so many times! Catch up to all of the thoughts! And to all of the preferences! Stop aching! Stop wailing! Stop weeping! Stop being hungry! Stop being full! Stop leaking and being gross! Be perfect! Be pure! Be clean! Be silent! Be dead, maybe!

Camille talked to Holly about workplaces in other parts of the world that honour women's hormonal cycles, and how they do their planning and strategising in the pre-ovulation phase, and they have meetings and presentations during the ovulation phase, before they plough into reviewing and rearranging during the pre-menstrual phase, and then they stop to reflect during the menstrual phase. Holly took this personally, as if Camille were implying that Florals wasn't progressive or sensitive enough, which it's not. Not when you consider how progressive or sensitive it *could* be. I mean, siestas are deemed reasonable by entire nations of people. But Holly rolled her eyes and was like, 'hun, if you wanna be babied, go and work for some mother hen, 'cos I'm about making it in the *real world*. I'm not interested in airy-fairy alternative universes.'

Never mind that when some online women's-media outlet is interviewing Holly, and asking her about her work ethic, she'll throw words like 'holistic' and 'collaborative' and 'flow' around as if she knows what they mean, because she's smart enough to know that she needs to seem smart enough to know, you know.

A year or so ago, Holly got a dating app and she started communicating with a much younger guy. Camille never met him or saw a photo, but she liked to imagine him as a bit of a dandy. Maybe an angular Scorpio with brooding tendencies. Holly's excitement about him was intoxicating. But she and Lover Boy couldn't nail down a time to meet in person, so they were messaging heaps, and she was giggling at her desk most days. She'd barely touch her chicken Caesar salads.

She'd read out Lover Boy's messages and Camille would help her to write replies. Camille showed her how to send gifs. She upgraded her emojis. Holly tried different ways of dressing, too. She'd always return to the safety of denim-on-denim, but Camille got to see Holly in a dress on this particularly fresh spring day. It was a salmon-coloured crepe de chine wraparound Diane von Furstenberg number with an orchid print. Holly took off her wedding ring for the first time since she'd gotten divorced and she put on these tiny gold stackable rings that a friend had given her for her fiftieth. Then, she paraded up and down High Street so that her ex-husband would see. She claimed she had to 'go to the bank' several times for no clearly discernible reason — and her ex *did* see. Apparently, he 'completely deconstructed' at the sight of her, and Camille was not surprised by this at all. Holly has a genuine magnetism and zest for life that can infect those around her. Like any good villain, she isn't 'all bad'. There's magic in Maleficent.

So it's sad that the whole thing with Lover Boy ended up being an act that lasted a few weeks, if that. Holly went on a date with him and, to this day, Camille doesn't know what happened. Holly took sick leave the following week, and Camille hoped her absence was due to the fact she'd been swallowed up by a gooey love nest with the guy in some hotel room, and that she was busy ordering French fries she wouldn't normally eat, and eating banana fritters she wouldn't normally look at, but Camille knew that this probably wasn't the case. So she started taking adaptogens in preparation for Holly's return, even though nothing could prepare her for what was to come.

There was an unprecedented heatwave that December, which is really saying something in Australia. But not even the consistently hot weather could slow Holly down or empty Armadale's streets pre-Christmas and during wedding season. The roads were steaming, bright, and buzzing with brides-to-be. Florals had weddings and office Christmas parties booked, which had been on the schedule for months, but then, at the last minute, Holly decided to offer more events at a cheaper rate. Then it was like, 'Camille? Didn't we deal with that already?' And 'haven't you called the fake-flowers guy back since this morning?' And 'where is the order for the blown-glass vases?' And 'the peonies were meant to be delivered by now. Follow up.' And 'you're having a break? Can't you wait half an hour?' And 'wasn't Georgia in the warehouse today? Didn't you message her when I asked you to?' And 'why did you tell the girls to start preparing this afternoon's order now, Camille? The truck for this morning's job will be *HERE IN A MINUTE.*'

Camille wondered if Holly was doing cocaine. The woman would never admit it, but the big Dust would definitely be her drug of choice. She claims to have been a flower child, or one of those purple children — *Indigo children* — because Holly would like to think that weed or LSD or molly or magic mushrooms were her thing, but she's way too much of a control freak to ingest anything that might get in the way of her being able to manoeuvre things in the way that she wants.

It was late on a Wednesday when Camille blurted out that it might be good to hire another pair of hands during December to help with coordinating all of the drivers' in-and-out of the warehouse, because that was the main difficulty for Georgia and Alyce: the laneway at the back of the building is narrow, and there needs to be some kind of road patrol to help the drivers get in and out, and Holly almost slapped her. And by then she'd put her wedding ring back on, too, so.

If she'd slapped Camille, it would've hurt like a bitch.

Holly reflects the part of Camille that wants to slap Camille.

AU

Camille really wanted to stop smoking weed. She wanted a
Hot Girl Summer. She wanted things to be different, and she
blamed marijuana for them not being. So she stopped rolling
a joint in the evenings and completely lost the plot. Lola and
Pope wouldn't go near her. Manny couldn't say anything right.
Her eyes were puffy in the mornings, and she couldn't tell if
it was from tears, or from fury, or from gluten. She couldn't
remember anything about the day, the week, or the night
before. Had Christmas happened? Had she snapped at Georgia
again? Wailed in her sleep? Or when she was talking to Manny?
It made Camille wonder where tears even come from

    and

    like

    why do people cry?

    Like

    why did people *evolve* to cry?

    What evolutionary purpose does it serve?

One night, she screamed into her pillow and beat the bed en route to the shower and she had visions of tearing Florals apart

one foot in front of the other

a knight in shining armour

goodbye buckets, goodbye computer, goodbye vases, goodbye display boxes, goodbye flowers, goodbye frames, no hard feelings and all of that, only soft feelings as you're smashed to bits

where are you? Who are you? What is this place? How did you get here? Who cares? Why is it hilarious? What the fuck is going on? What are all of these words, and images, and dreams, and fears, and feelings even *MADE OF*?

MUSCLES?

BAHAHAAAAA

YEAH

SURE

WHATEVER

JUST REMEMBER

THIS IS NED KELLY COUNTRY YOU FUCKING COW

HAVE SOME FUCKING RESPECT

Camille started smoking weed again. She couldn't live without any sense of reward for her efforts — so she resorted to what gave her instant gratification.

And, day by day, she became more comfortable with the idea of herself as a weed smoker than as a woman who loves and works with flowers. Being a weed smoker highlighted what was social and chill about Camille, rather than what was weird and demanding. So she sank into her habit once again. She sat back, relaxed, smoked a joint — or knew that she could smoke a joint later — and she laughed, and she avoided her feelings, and her dreams, because that's what everyone else was avoiding, too. Then Camille felt like she was a part of something, even if it was at the expense of her soul, and the souls of other people.

Flowers might be the enlightened beings of the plant world, but Camille convinced herself that those around her would only care about her love of flowers, fragrances, and flower essences when she became a zillionaire or an internet sensation from working with them. Until then, she's a try-hard, and maybe a flake, who really needs to get a grip, because no one knows a goddamn thing about something like *flower essences*. Or, if they do, they associate them with harem pants, and with bare feet pitter-pattering around the supermarket, and with forager vibes, and with healing modalities that 'don't work'.

A couple of months ago, Camille was lining up a few new flower-essence blends in a sunny spot on the windowsill in the kitchen, and she caught Manny watching her from where he was watering the garden, and she looked away, because she still feels self-conscious about who she is and what she wants, even though Manny can see who she is and what she wants, and he loves her for it. But he can't force her to embrace it. He can only water the flowers and wait for her to choose them.

Because Camille refuses to see herself as anything more than a woman who smokes weed like a badass bitch and works for the famous Holly Hughes. She's a woman who follows orders, and aims to please, and to slowly acquire promotions, despite all of the evidence to suggest that there will be no promotions and no pleasing. She's a woman who consents to emotional beatings from her boss because she's convinced herself that they're warranted. She's a woman who thinks her place in the scheme of things doesn't involve a wild and unstoppable healing force that has the power to create worlds and to transform the world around her; a wild and unstoppable healing force that reconciles human beings with the universe that they inhabit. The universe *that they are made of*. No, no.

Camille is too busy slapping herself in the face.

Camille has made her way to Platform 10 and she's at war with her uterus. Men never seem to be at war with their penises. Penises, and all of their unique preferences, seem to run the world. The occasional boner might be awkward, but it isn't drugged and forced to stop doing what it was born to do. Camille's uterus creates humans, futures, galaxies, and she's expected to fight its inherent cycles, and to alter them, and to evade them. Her body is expected to be at-the-ready whenever the workday begins and whenever a penis might want to dip its tip into it.

Like *on Valentine's Day*.

Manny and Camille have never had sex when she's On the Rag. He'd probably be down for it if she was, but she's not. Everything in and around her vagina feels sensitive during that time and she needs total control over it. If she and Manny were to have sex, it would need to be slow, which isn't out of the question. Camille and Manny's sex life has become deeper and richer the longer that their relationship has had time to develop, which is in total opposition to the whole idea of a 'honeymoon period' and everything going downhill after it. The sex that Manny and Camille had at the start of their relationship was all hot and bothered. Clunky and awkward. Over the years, they've sunk into a much smoother tempo. A much deeper rhythm. They know each other's favourite positions, body parts, and angles. They use condoms, and Camille enjoys choosing the flavours. They know they're each other's chosen ones, for now. So they can relax.

Sex can feel a bit mechanical sometimes, though, and Camille gets an urge to try different things. Or at least she likes the *idea* of trying different things. She's not sure if she really wants to. The urge to try different things can be a swift road to discontent rather than a path to genuine gratification and exploration. It's better when new positions and ways of communicating through sex emerge naturally. When they're consciously sought after, sex can feel jarring and forced. Manny also needs to be a winner at everything, and Camille is an impatient beginner, so. Now that they've discovered mutually satisfying ways of interacting physically, they're quite attached to them, and it's probably best not to futz about with that too much. It's like a good sleeper reading about sleep techniques and becoming an insomniac. If it ain't broke, don't fix it.

Camille has two positions she slips into when she's masturbating, and she doesn't venture too far from these during sex, either. Their familiarity allows her to unlock completely. Then Camille can become excited about sex in an authentic way, rather than being nervous and scared on some level. Like, 'is it going to be good?' And 'how long is it going to go on for?' And 'is it going to make me orgasm?' And 'is it going to make *him* orgasm?' And 'what do I do if he doesn't orgasm?' And 'what do I do if I don't orgasm?' And 'will our relationship survive a lack of orgasm?' And 'that tantra lady said not to focus on orgasm, but *ORGASM ORGASM ORGASM*.'

Camille's cramps have got her thinking about sex, because sex is life, and life is sex, and the act of touching herself can loosen up her uterus, and get the blood flowing, and allow the tension to start dissolving. But, obviously, that isn't an option right now — Camille being late for work because she was attempting to get herself off in some dank and festy public toilet isn't exactly the picture of a morning commute well-executed.

Camille's mum, Jane, struggled with period pain as a teenager, but it went away after childbirth. Clarice used to stay home from school because of migraines. A girl that Camille met in a 'Romanticism, Feminism, and Revolution' lecture at Melbourne Uni had super-painful periods. She was diagnosed with endometriosis and she had surgery. Doctors hung her upside down and blew up her stomach with gas before they operated on her. A few of Camille's friends stay on the pill in order to avoid cramps and acne. One girl takes downers to get through PMS.

A nutritionist once told Camille that how smoothly she digests food is a big part of how smoothly the uterine lining sheds, and that the body's processes of elimination are all connected. Then, a herbalist Camille saw observed that she'd never met a woman that didn't experience some kind of disruption, or pain, around her Moon Time. It might be cramps, it might be migraines, it might be neck tension, it might be rage, it might be heartache — it all has the same energetic signature.

Camille used to take over-the-counter painkillers at work,

but she ran out a couple of months ago and just ... didn't buy more. They were on special at the supermarket the other day, and she thought about buying them, but something stopped her. Maybe she'd be ok without them, she thought. Maybe she'd buy some on the day if she needed them. Or, maybe, without them, her world would come undone. And maybe, deep down, that's what she wants.

One time, at a music festival, Camille found herself talking to This Older Woman. This Older Woman was wearing a kaftan, and she had bright-white hair that curled to the base of her spine. She was wearing silver jewellery around her neck, and along her arms, and it tinkled whenever she moved and gestured with her hands. Camille and This Older Woman were waiting to buy young coconuts — the ones you drink — and Camille ended up in a conversation with her about menstruation, because of course she did. Then This Older Woman told Camille that period pain is the collective feminine crying out in anguish. It's a call for the earth's inhabitants to slow down, and to become more receptive, and nurturing. To embrace darkness, stillness, and the unknown.

Because everyone wants to return to the womb.

Camille uses a menstrual cup. She stopped using tampons because cups seemed more economical, and better for the environment, and more sustainable. You can also put them in for eight hours rather than panicking after four. They're made from medical-grade silicone. Thick, unforgiving, yet flexible latex rubber. To insert The Cup, you have to squeeze it in half between your fingers, and slip it up and in. Then it expands like a flower, sticks to the walls of the vagina, and sits there catching blood. To get it out, you need to put your index and/ or middle fingers inside the vagina and unstick the silicone from the vaginal walls with a circling motion. There's also a bit of silicone that sticks out the bottom of The Cup like a stem, and after releasing the suction from the vaginal walls, you quickly pull the stem, whip it out, and empty the blood into the sink, or into the toilet, or wherever.

It's not easy to manage in public toilets, though. If the blood is particularly thick when you pull The Cup out, there might be a heavy string of it dangling there, between The Cup and your vagina, which you then have to break up with your fingers, or with toilet paper, otherwise it'll drip onto your clothes, or onto the floor, or onto the toilet seat. Then you have to emerge from the cubicle with bloodstained fingers, which you may feel inclined to hide en route to the basin to wash your hands.

Camille had this particular Cup for a year or so. She doesn't really know how long menstrual cups are supposed to last. She assumed it would outlive her, as so many man-made things have the capacity to do. And Camille kept Manny away from the monthly machinations of The Cup. Consciously, but not consciously. The two of them wee and poop with the door open. They keep chatting, etc. But when The Cup would come into play, Manny would excuse himself, or Camille might let him know, 'hey, I'm doing my Cup now', and he'd be like 'ok' and disappear.

There were a couple of times when Camille was doing The Cup — either putting it in or pulling it out — and she thought that she could hear Manny coming up the stairs and she quickly sat down on the toilet again, which was a bit weird. Like, why did she do that? Why did she try to hide The Cup from Manny? Why did she feel complete and utter terror when he might be about to witness her putting in or taking The Cup out?

Then, one Sunday, she innocently went upstairs to do her thing with The Cup. She propped her leg up on the side of the bathtub, performed the usual swirling motion with her middle finger, went to pull The Cup out, and the stem snapped. It took a minute for Camille to recognise the implications of this. There was some shock to digest before she could cognitively grasp the fact that The Cup was now inside her. Sans stem.

Therefore
   no way
   to get Cup
   out.

It goes pretty high up into the vagina, too. The Cup gets very cosy with the cervix, and the suction between it and the vaginal walls is strong. Industrial strong. You really need the combination of the swirling motion of your fingers and the pulling-down motion of the stem to get it to exit the body with ease. Miss a step and there is no ease. And no exit.

Camille had a hot flush. She could hear Manny downstairs listening to Alice Coltrane and doing last night's dishes. The tap turned on and the tap turned off. There was scrubbing and the squirting of detergent. Eventually, she made her way down to him.

'I think I need your help.'

'Ok?'

'With my menstrual Cup.'

'Ok.'

'It's stuck."

'Stuck how?'

'Do you know what it looks like?'

'Umm.'

'It's, like, a Cup, with a pull-y-out-y thing. It's made of silicone. It's held up there by suction. And the pull-y-out-y thing, like, broke. I don't know why. Or how. A lot of pulling goes on each month, I guess. I wash it and everything. But, umm, I can't get it out. Like, I can't get at it vigorously enough myself. You might have more ... pull. With two hands. Or something.'

'Alright. Does it need to happen now?'

'No. Although. I'll probably need to go to the doctor to, like, get it extracted or whatever if neither of us can get it out.'

'Oh.'

'Yeah.'

'Ok. I'll just finish the dishes and then. Yep.'

Camille drifted over to the coffee table and picked up a book on Greek architecture and tried to seem laid-back about things. But when you notice yourself trying to seem laid-back about things, you probably aren't laid-back about things. Nevertheless, Camille proceeded with this course of action, hoping it would eventually lead her to feeling laid-back about things, and it did. Kind of.

The reality of the situation only set in again when Manny dried his hands and walked over to Camille. Then he raised his eyebrows, shrugged his shoulders, took a shallow breath, and gestured toward the stairs in an almost chivalrous manner, indicating that they should ascend to the bathroom now. Camille dutifully did so, and as she moved upstairs, she wondered why the whole ordeal felt so horrifying. The horror of it on a physical level was obvious. However, the horror of it on mental, emotional, and spiritual levels was more elusive to her.

Camille couldn't grasp the exact reason she'd kept Manny away from The Cup or why needing his help with it was so humiliating. 'Hiding it is just what you do' came to mind. 'Uphold the mystery' came to mind. 'It's a personal preference' came to mind. 'Boundaries' came to mind. 'So that he doesn't think less of you' came to mind. Yet Camille couldn't think of a bodily function that Manny shrouded in secrecy to the same extent. So she wondered about where her shame came from. Especially given the fact that half of the planet's human population has, will have, or once had, a period. Most men are dealing with women dealing with periods. Then Camille's inner eye saw plagues and churches. Something old that wasn't hers.

Camille propped her leg back up on the corner of the bathtub. Manny squatted, slightly, with his hands at the ready under her vagina, and his gaze over her left shoulder, as her gaze drifted over his left shoulder. He didn't crack a joke. He didn't groan. He didn't get angry. He furrowed his brow. He breathed in and out of his nostrils steadily. Yet even with two hands and a whole lot of fingers, Manny couldn't nail the swishing-and-pulling motion. Well, he nailed it once. He almost pulled The Cup out, but Camille got scared about Manny seeing blood in his hands, and she clenched, and The Cup shot straight back up toward her cervix.

Then Manny washed his hands and they agreed to take a timeout. Camille returned to admiring whitewashed walls with blue accents and Manny escaped to the garden where Camille suspected he was fixing the backyard hose with gaffer tape again. The dogs looked on from their respective cushions, and at one point Pope approached Camille, sniffed her, and returned to his bed.

The second time, as they ascended the stairs, Camille started to worry that a trip to the GP might be required after all. Camille hates going to the doctors. Authority figures of all kinds have started to trouble her. Even the *concept* of an authority figure has started to trouble her. Because Camille requires Manny's help right now. So, is he the authority figure? Because she asked him for help? And because he has more physical strength than she does? And a better angle to get around her hoo-ha? Or is Camille the authority figure? Because it's her body and her choice? Or is there no such thing as an authority figure? Because you're either helping each other or you're not?

During round two, Manny breathed even louder through his nose. He quit looking over Camille's shoulder. He focused his attention upon his hands. He squatted and he pulled. He twisted with his fingers, and his concentration, and care, allowed Camille's body to open. And then, with a gasp, the bloody Cup saw the light.

Camille is finally on the train to Armadale. She's slid into a seat facing the opposite way from the direction the train is going in because she prefers travelling backwards and falling into the future. She's shut her eyes. She can see a bright-red rope in the darkness. It's wrapped around her pelvis, hip flexors, and uterus. It keeps getting tighter and tighter, then releasing slightly, before tightening again. It has a pulse. It's a hand gripping her insides. It's clenched. Stiff. Refusing to let go. Camille wants to massage it and to ask it to be more gentle. Tears are welling up in her eyes. Breathe. Breathe. What station is this? South Yarra. Ok, three more stops. Sink into the seat

   down

   down

   through the train tracks

   into the rocks

   around the roots

through the soil
into the black cool damp
soak in the nutrients
it's ok
everything is going to be ok

Camille was first introduced to relaxation and visualisation techniques by her grandmother Jacqueline. Jacqueline lived on a big block of land in Elwood, near the beach. It was an olive-coloured one-storey Victorian homestead. It had white lattice windows and wind chimes. There was an older dog that looked like a dingo, and a black cat called Oscar that would sprint around, and claw at tree trunks, and roll in the dirt. There were veggie patches, herbs, fig trees, and flowers. Peonies, boronias, lilly pillies, rhododendrons, gardenias, grevilleas, camellias, nasturtiums, kangaroo paws, marigolds, wild lavender, daisies, and snapdragons.

Whenever Camille spent an afternoon with Jacqueline as a child, and it was time to eat, the two of them would venture out into the garden. They'd pick whatever was in season — tomatoes, mixed lettuce leaves, nasturtiums, a lemon, and some mint for cups of tea, which Jacqueline would serve in a gold Moroccan tea set on a tray on the verandah. There was a beehive down the back of the property, too. Although the bees scared Camille, this didn't stop her from enjoying at least three teaspoons of Jacqueline's honey in the mint teas. Eventually, Jacqueline nicknamed Camille 'Honey Bee', because Jacqueline was of the belief that people's fears were to be cherished like loved ones.

Paintings and photographs adorned every room in Jacqueline's house. She collected big seashells and stuck them to the walls between the pictures. Large geranium candles filled empty spaces alongside hunks of smoky quartz, howlite, and obsidian obelisks as big as your arm. Bunches of dried hydrangeas hung from wooden beams in the kitchen, and the only harp Camille has ever seen in real life was the one in the corner of Jacqueline's lounge room.

When Camille visited in the afternoons, she would help Jacqueline in the garden. They both loved pruning and weeding in the rain. Or Jacqueline would be in the study, doing things on the computer and talking in French on the phone. Jacqueline had worked in France as an advertising executive before she moved to Australia to be with Camille's grandfather Marcus. The two of them travelled around Australia a lot, so photos of them camping in the bush and walking across different deserts and climbing different rocks were scattered throughout the house. They adored Byron Bay.

Marcus was a dynamic-looking man with thick sandy hair and a square jaw. In every photo, he seems to be smoking a pipe and wearing khaki pants and long-sleeved shirts. He was a barrister. And he worked hard. Very hard. He died under mysterious circumstances in his sixties. Well, they weren't entirely mysterious. Marcus drove his Saab into a tree in the middle of a court case involving children, parents, and murder. At family gatherings, people quietly refer to his death as 'The

Crash' before they change the subject. Camille never met him. And when Camille was a child, that didn't matter. The only thing she cared about was going to Jacqueline's, and spending time with her, and with the harp, and with the flowers. It was only when she got older that she became more curious about Marcus and the similarities she, Clarice, and Jane might have with him.

And it was sitting in Jacqueline's study that Camille first learned about Dreamtime. At school, she'd come away from classes about Australian history assuming that Dreamtime was a literal, historical time and place, billions of years ago. That it was a static, lost entity. But between the pages of books at Jacqueline's house, Camille began to understand that there was more to Dreamtime. Maybe it was, and is, everything. Maybe trees, flowers, rocks, sticks, dirt, insects, oceans, rivers, sun, moon, stars, mountains, air, fruits, vegetables, animals, and minerals are Dreamtime. Maybe Camille's ancestors are Dreamtime. Maybe the past, present, and future are Dreamtime.

Maybe Camille is Dreamtime.

Camille was in Jacqueline's bedroom when they did a meditation together for the first time. It was one of those freezing, bleak days in May, and Camille was flu-ey and upset. She had flat-out refused to go to school, and when Jane had said that she'd take her to Jacqueline's, Camille didn't want to go. She wanted to stay at home and watch cartoons, but no one was around.

When Jane dropped Camille off at Jacqueline's, Camille couldn't look Jacqueline in the eye. Jacqueline had deep, knowing eyes. So as the two women were talking, Camille stared at Jacqueline's wooden clogs and light-brown woollen socks, which she wore around the house. Then Jane backed out of the driveway, and Jacqueline took a sulking Camille by the hand. They walked along the wooden floorboards to Jane's bedroom, which was Camille's least favourite room in the house. It was draughty and bare.

Jacqueline instructed Camille to lie down on the bed. She

added patchouli, bergamot, ylang ylang, and sweet orange essential oils to a burner, which sat on the bedside table. Then she lit the candle, opened the windows, and drew the curtains. Jacqueline sat down on an old trunk at the end of the bed, put her hands around the iron bars of the frame, and whispered, 'Ow-k. Lay down. Lizzen to may voiss. Led de worrrrlt mult eway.'

And it did.

Jacqueline died on a Saturday. The weather was clear. It's strange to think that people die on sunny days — not even the sun in all its glory can stop it.

Jacqueline never had her physical ailments checked. She often repeated the phrase 'happy, healthy, dead' and that's pretty much how it went. On the one occasion she did go to a physician, they told her that she had cancer, and that she should undergo treatment immediately, so Jacqueline said 'au revoir!' and rode home on her bike. She didn't tell anyone for years. It was only when she and Camille were clearing autumn leaves from the gutters that she happened to mention it. And she mentioned it in passing, as if they'd talked about it before. Like, *so* many times. *Very* boring now.

Camille was aghast. Did she have symptoms? Did she worry? Did she think the family should know? Did Jane know? 'Non, non, non, et non.' Then Jacqueline mumbled something in French about how resenting Marcus had taken a toll on her, before she waved her hand like a wand and declared that she didn't want to discuss any of it ever again.

Camille was the one who found her. She visited Jacqueline most Saturday mornings for a cup of mint tea and a croissant before going to work at the florist on Johnston Street. Jacqueline would buy Camille the latest issue of French *Vogue* and lay it out on the kitchen table along with a small jar of honey, Lescure butter, and blackberry jam. Then she'd turn on Classic FM and keep the croissants warm in the oven until Camille arrived.

She died in her sleep. The windows were open. The curtains were drawn. The bedroom smelled like frankincense. She was wearing mint-green silk pyjamas, and the house was still except for the wind chimes outside.

Camille kissed Jacqueline on the forehead and sat at the end of the bed. She thought about friends of hers who'd gone through family members dying in hospitals and in aged-care homes. She looked at Jacqueline lying there, and memories of all her ways of doing things, and of all her ways of seeing things, moved through Camille like smoke

like dust

like stars.

Camille was devastated when Jane decided to sell the Elwood house. It felt like a violation beyond mere sentiment. Interest rates are rising, money is basically becoming obsolete, land is everything, water is life, plants are food, food is love, love is earth, and on, and on. Camille worried that Jane was selling the place because she grew up feeling embarrassed to have a foreign mother who would go to weekend markets, and buy wind chimes, and stick flora and fauna all over the walls of her house, because 'pourquoi pas, ma chérie?'

Jane manages a bookshop in Richmond. She wears cotton shirts and tailored trousers. She doesn't own wind chimes. She reads the paper every day and she loves sudoku and crossword puzzles. Joan Didion is her favourite writer. She struggles with Manny's poetry. It's so sparse and abstract; she wishes he would lighten up a bit. Yet she insists on pretending that she likes his work, and she goes to great lengths to appear a fan, and she puts his book in the window of the shop and, much to her surprise, it sells ok.

Jane understands French, but she doesn't speak it. Camille was angry about this as a teenager, because she wanted to seem exotic to her classmates, but Jane couldn't help.

Jane runs a book club with her girlfriends, and they don't all read the same book. Sometimes they don't read books at all. Instead, they bring interesting articles they've come across, or cookbooks they've found, because the real aim of the occasion is to laugh, and to cry, and to process what's happening in their lives and relationships. They sip gin and tonics, and eat green-bean salads, and platters of oysters — for the zinc! for the zinc! — and a special Croatian dish one of them makes with calamari and soft cheese.

Jane married Camille's dad in her early twenties, and she doesn't regret it. But she *is* a Gemini with a Cancer moon, so there's definitely more to Jane than crossword puzzles, tailored slacks, and contentment. For one thing, Camille and Jane have exhausted one another ever since Camille's conception in the wet tropics of Queensland, which also happens to be the home of some of the world's most ancient flowering plants. Camille was restless in the womb. Labour was challenging, because Camille refused to do what the doctors wanted her to. She simply wouldn't get into the appropriate position. So she entered the world in 'breech' and on the verge of being a caesarean baby and, now, whenever Camille and Jane talk on the phone, there's a sense of escalation and panic that neither of them can explain.

Jane, Camille, and Clarice went through Jacqueline's house together. Camille claimed the distiller, and the Moroccan tea set, and Marcus's golden pipe, and an obsidian obelisk, and some shells, and the wind chimes, and several books on Australia. The harp wouldn't fit in the car. She asked her parents if she and Manny could rent the place and they said no. Well, they said they'd think about it, which usually means they'll go away and act as if they're discussing the matter further, because they'd like to think of themselves as being open-minded, reasonable people, but then they'll return with the same answer they gave initially.

No.

So, one night, Camille smoked some skunky weed that she found in the kitchen pantry and she tried to speak to Jane about why she was selling the house over the phone, before she tripped out right in the middle of the relatively high-stakes conversation.

Yes, right in the middle of Jane pulling rank, and trying to sound authoritative as she explained to her youngest daughter the practicalities of caring for a house, which clearly wasn't something Camille could be expected to understand, because she wasn't a home owner yet, Camille experienced this meta-view of herself, and of Jane, and of Clarice, and of Jacqueline. She saw all of their hopes and dreams being passed down through the ether. And it occurred to her that what children have to teach their parents is so much more valuable than what parents have to teach their children, because while parents give their children tools for survival, children guard their parents' souls.

'So does that make sense?'

'Um.'

'What would you have us do, Camille?'

'I'm sorry, but I can't just be like, "oh, ok, that's fine," because it doesn't feel right.'

'Look I know how close you were to Mum and how much that place means to you. I do. I love it, too. But there's so much she didn't attend to, and your father and I can barely keep on top of the work we need to do at our place. Old houses are ... difficult.'

'Is it because you resent Jacqueline still? Or because you resent me?'

'*Camille.*'

'I don't know, ok? I don't know. I just don't want to say goodbye to it for the wrong reasons, Mum.'

'Well, I'm sorry that my reasoning seems unconvincing to you, Camille, but it also happens to be a good time to sell.'

'Right.'

'Hopefully you'll understand one day?'

'I "understand" now, Mum. It just doesn't feel right.'

Camille definitely needs a coffee from Lord Byron before she gets to Florals.

There are two sides to Armadale Station: the one that leads to the shops, where Florals is, and the one that takes you down winding, tree-lined walkways, past well-kept rose bushes, iron gates, trimmed hedges, tiled front porches, leadlight windows, and dog walkers. This is the side of Armadale Station that Lord Byron is on. It's a narrow, angular old building, which moulds itself to the shape of the corner it's built upon. It has big square windows and glossy wooden floors. It has naked lightbulbs hanging from the ceiling, which is high. Outside, there are rows of white tables, white chairs, and white-and-yellow striped umbrellas.

And it's a sight to behold this morning: lots of bodies in singlets crammed into it. It's quite a bit to navigate, but Camille is very set on coffee, so she has deemed it worth the effort. She also has to negotiate a way to *not* pay for coffee, because she doesn't have her phone. And she'll have to figure out a way to *not* pay for a skinny latte for Holly if she's going to *not* pay for a soy cap for herself, because Holly gets shitty if Camille arrives at work with a coffee and hasn't got one for her, too. Holly never finishes the coffees Camille gets for her, though, because she loves going down to Lord Byron by herself, and flirting with Seamus. Every Monday she arrives as he starts his shift so that she can be the first to ask him about how his weekend was, and then she can voyeur into his sexcapades, and feel disappointed she wasn't a part of them, and envious of the women who were.

Seamus is Irish, and an actor, and a waiter, and a model, and a musician. He flirts with everyone, and everything, and Holly doesn't like it when Camille makes jokes about this. Holly wants to feel like Seamus's special someone. So she'll hardly drink the coffee Camille feels obligated to get for her before she'll head down to see Seamus, and to get another coffee, which she'll also hardly drink. Camille's not sure Holly even likes coffee. She just wants to be sophisticated and involved in things. But Seamus loves the attention. His days at Lord Byron revolve around entertaining women like Holly. Camille saw him moving his car one time, and it was an old van with an assortment of stickers on the back window, and one of them said 'MILF WHISPERER'.

Seamus has a square face, a strong brow, and curly hair. His smile is enormous, and he exploits it. He has green eyes, and he wears buttoned-down shirts that reveal a broad, well-worked chest. Last summer, he added a thin silver chain with a locket into the mix, and it drove Holly mad. 'Who do you think gave it to him?' And 'it's very feminine?' And 'doesn't it accentuate his eyes?' And *'DID YOU NOTICE THAT THE LOCKET IS GONE? OOOO I WONDER WHAT HAPPENNNNDDDDD.'*

Seamus used to lean over the counter when Camille ordered their takeaway coffees, and when she picked up Holly's daily chicken Caesar salads, and he'd be like, 'come on, babe, it's never too early in the day for Prosecco?' And 'going out tonight? Can I come?' And 'not even a smile for me today, bella?', and Camille would just glare at him. So he doesn't bother with her anymore.

The one time Manny came into Florals — more about that later — he saw Seamus out the front of Lord Byron making a table full of private-school girls giggle, and blush, and fiddle with the loose hems of their skirts, and Manny was like, 'oh my *GOD* get *OVER* yourself and your *IDEAS* about shit, dude.'

Manny is classically handsome, too, but he's made a choice not to harness his powers of handsomeness to get ahead in the world, for better or for worse. Manny prefers to hide behind obscure poetry, and rich-poor pride, and a sense of himself as superior to others, because he hides from them in the country, and manages to uphold an air of mystery that only physical distance can provide. He has thick, oily dark hair, which he never attends to, and olive skin, and brown eyes, and broad shoulders. He looks like a farmer, even though he's not. His great-great-uncle on his dad's side was a farmer. Or maybe he ran an orchard? Or a winery? Camille can't remember. Either way, that's about as close to agriculture as Manny's family line gets. And he uses his smile sparingly. Too sparingly, some would say. 'Some' being Camille's parents. They think Manny and Camille look like River Phoenix and Martha Plimpton, and it concerns them. They find Manny too morose. But he's definitely the strangest, and the funniest, and the most glorious person Camille has ever met.

Lord Byron's barista, Amy, is much more Camille's style. She's on the coffee machine from 7am, before Seamus arrives, and she's into women, too, but she isn't gross about it, like Seamus. Amy smiles with her eyes and she never asks how Camille is or what she's been up to. She doesn't make an awkward point of Camille's being a regular. Camille only knows Amy's name because she happened to overhear one of the more transient teenage waitresses saying it when she was asking Amy for a saucer one time.

Amy has tattoos of a pomegranate on her wrist and a gold key on her upper arm. She also has a septum piercing. And an eyebrow ring. And who knows *what* else. It makes you wonder.

There are two women in exercise gear ordering before Camille, and Camille can't stop looking at their shapely shoulders and their perfectly sculpted butts. One of them is in a violet-coloured crop top and matching high-waisted lycra short shorts. The other is wearing a teal-coloured razorback singlet and she has her hair in a ponytail. There are beads of sweat around the base of her neck. They've both got tan lines from strappy swimsuits, and they're both scrolling on their phones, and Camille wishes that she could be scrolling on her phone, because sometimes when she sees other people scrolling on their phones, she feels compelled by some unseen force to do exactly the same.

'So she just RSVP'd through the form thing?'

'Yep.'

'Didn't call? Didn't text?'

'Nope.'

'No card? No gift?'

'I know. After all these years.'

'Wtf. I'm so sorry, sweet.'

Camille feels intimidated by people who clearly spend a lot of time focused on their physical bodies. She doesn't know how to do that without feeling guilty. So Camille chooses to care for herself less, because she's frightened of appearing as if she cares for herself too much — as if that were even possible.

Camille enjoys walking Lola and Pope with Manny. It takes forty minutes or so, but it doesn't push her. She's had gym memberships, and she likes doing weights, but she's never used the gym enough to justify paying the exorbitant fees. Then she started going to a sauna when she and Manny were still living in Melbourne, and she loved dripping with sweat and having a cold shower afterwards. It was detoxifying after a week with Holly. But a month or so into Camille's new routine, Holly needed her to work late, and then she and Manny moved to the country, so that was the end of that.

Camille's done pilates classes, and yoga classes, and ballet classes. But getting to a class at the allocated time, and finding a spot to park, or somewhere to tie up a bike, would take just as much energy as doing the class. Then the class would be crowded, because everyone was going before or after work. Then the teacher would change, or go on vacation, and their replacement would either be a dud, or their replacement would be better than them, and, either way, it would suck. Then there was the change-room etiquette, and the stinky feet, and the mirrors, and the wandering eyes.

Manny does sport with his mates whenever he can — soccer, tennis, golf, cycling, basketball, cricket — but there aren't as many opportunities anymore. Partly because he and

Camille live in the country, and partly because everyone's working and/or having babies now. And when there *are* opportunities to be sporty, the expectations are unclear. Like, is this socially or aerobically motivated? Are we pushing each other? Or are we just hanging out?

Manny and Camille would both benefit from more intense exercise, but neither of them do it. Even if human beings need resistance to grow, there's something so exposing about strenuous physical activity for the sake of strenuous physical activity. It's, like, 'umm, surely there's something better you could be doing?' And 'why bother when your technique probably sucks?' And 'careful, you'll prematurely wear out your joints.' And 'how're you going to maintain the fitness you gain, anyway? Are you going to keep at it?' And 'you're not an athlete so what's the point?' And 'couldn't you be doing laundry now? Or cooking a week's worth of meals?' And 'you just spent the day dealing with Holly. Aren't you exhausted?'

Camille has wanted to get back into running. Especially because, to run, all she needs to do is *go*. And if Camille had used half of the time she's spent wanting to run, running, she'd be super fit by now. She'd be like the women waiting in line in front of her: wearing exercise gear around the clock just in case the urge to *exert* overcame her. She'd be fierce. She'd fuck for hours. She'd be full of endorphins. She'd be able to move cumbersome furniture, and mulch, without having to take a break. She'd live on her terms.

One time, Camille was looking up the phone number for the local fish'n'chip shop on Manny's phone, and she noticed that he'd been looking at some sexy gifs in one of his tabs, and the sexy gifs involved women that looked a lot like the two currently standing in front of Camille. Strong. Toned. Hand jobs for days. Camille didn't find the images entirely displeasing, either. There was something relieving about them. Something that said, 'hey, you. I am a body. Time to fuck.'

Manny walked into the room to get the car keys and Camille found herself saying something to him about the gifs. She hadn't planned to, but Mercury was in retrograde and her mouth opened.

'Well, these are a bit sexy.'

'Oh.'

'You don't have to say anything.'

'Ok.'

'But did you, like, jerk off to them?'

'Shit, Camille.'

'I get turned on by gifs sometimes, too.'

'That's nice.'

'It's true.'

'Ok, but just because *you're* talking about it doesn't mean I have to.'

'True.'

'And, like, those gifs are pretty pedestrian in the scheme of things.'

'You mean in the scheme of things you *could* be looking at?'

'Yeah. I dunno. Yeah.'

'So do you think about these kinds of women when we're having sex?'

'Are we really doing this now? I think the fish'n'chip place closes at 8pm.'

'They're open till 8.30pm in the summer.'

'Are you sure?'

'Yes.'

'You don't need to check?'

'No.'

'Ok.'

'Ok.'

'I'm gonna be really pissed if we get there and they're shut.'

'They won't be shut.'

'Ok.'

'Well?'

'Well, what?'

'Well, do you think about these kinds of women when we're having sex?'

'What do you mean by "these kinds of women"?'

'I don't know how else to say it.'

'Do *you* think about these kinds of women when we're having sex?'

'Are you seriously answering a question with a question?'

'Yes.'

'Fine. Ok. I have imagined myself being stronger, and having a bigger butt, and bigger boobs, when we're having sex. The other night, I had a dream that I became Kylie Jenner, and after I had got over the corporeal reality of having had, like, large amounts of silicon sewn into different parts of my body, all I wanted was to get your attention, and to fuck.'

'Ok?'

'And, you know, sometimes when I touch myself, I imagine you with women that look a bit like this and I get turned on by it. But the idea of you *actually* being with other women before my *actual* eyes is kind of perturbing, though. So. Not sure what that's about.'

'I still don't really know what to say.'

'That's ok.'

'Is it?'

'Yeah. Maybe I just needed to talk about it.'

'Ok. Can we order now? Or, what am I supposed to say?'

'Nothing, I guess.'

'I just ... Being fit is sexy.'

'I agree.'

'But your body is amazing.'

'Thank you. I wasn't asking for that, necessarily, but I appreciate it, if you mean it, and if you're not just saying that now in the context of what we're talking about, because you think that my starting a dialogue about sexual desire and, like, fitness, is due to the fact that I'm insecure.'

'Shit, Camille.'

'It's ok, ok? Never mind. Onward. Chips. Whatever. I don't even want to talk about it anymore.'

'I love your body.'

'Thanks. I could be fitter, though. Not for, like, sexual reasons. Although that part of my life — and that part of our lives — would probably benefit from both of us being fitter.

Not that our sex life *needs* that.'

'I know. Me too. It's all good.'

'Yeah?'

'Yeah, ok. And let's not get the chips well-done tonight.'

'Good idea.'

'Yeah, they made me feel sick last time.'

The coffees are taking longer this morning, because of course they are. Amy is inundated. And Camille felt bad having to negotiate with her about paying for the coffees later, even though Amy was a good sport about it.

So Camille has woven her way outside, because she's got nothing to do in this hectic social environment, which is a perilous state to find oneself in. Without anything to do. Publicly. And it's in moments like these, which rarely occur, that Camille fantasises about being calm; about being present. About taking in the moment fully.

Sometimes when Camille and Manny are high, and they're watching an animated movie, like *Sleeping Beauty*, Camille will realise that she hasn't had a thought in ages. Aurora will be waltzing across the screen, laughing with her owl friend, and singing 'I know you / I walked with you once upon a dream' to the prince, and Camille won't be thinking about anything. She'll just be watching. And then she'll notice herself just watching, and life will seem worth living.

Camille tried to talk about this with Manny, but the subject made him tense. He was like, 'yeah, sorry, but, ah, that "not thinking" and "not feeling" and "being neutral" crap is some of the most inhumane shit I've ever heard,' before he returned to pulling tiny weeds out from around the snapdragons. Camille went on to say that neutrality didn't mean becoming numb, necessarily, but her words petered out, and evaporated into the air, and sank into the soil, and started to fertilise the plants, because Manny couldn't really hear her after that.

A friend of Manny's once came over with his girlfriend for a barbecue — when Manny and Camille were still eating meat — and Friend of Manny's entered the building holding a massive uncooked lamb roast that he'd marinaded in garlic, sage, soy sauce, and chilli oil. Then he'd cut up all of these onions to put on the barbecue with it, and as he unloaded the carcass onto the kitchen bench, he was like, 'Yep, didn't shed *A SINGLE TEAR* when I was cutting up all of these onions, eh.'

Camille widened her eyes in the direction of irony, or some kind of relief she began to sense she wasn't going to get, before he followed up by insisting that, 'seriously, not a drop.' Then he added, 'and there are, at least, like ... what? Ten onions in here?' His girlfriend then proceeded to hum in agreement, and to pat him on the back, and Camille couldn't work out if she'd slipped into congratulating him for this noble feat because she could see how desperately he needed said congratulations, or because she wanted the whole thing to stop, and to go away, or if she seriously thought her boyfriend was a hero for how he had handled the onions, and she wanted to be associated with him in a clearly delineated way. So Camille laughed.

And her laughter was interpreted as admiration.

Maybe LB's staff don't know where Camille is. Or they feel awkward about coming outside to give her the coffees because it's busy. Or they resent her for not paying yet. Regardless, Camille is now worried about being late for work. That'd be right. Holly would love for Camille to make an obvious mistake like being late on such a crazy day. Then she wouldn't have to go out of her way to scold Camille: she'd be handed the opportunity to do so on a plate.

Being late would also create such an unfortunate opening for, like, 'oh, you're late. Everything ok at *home*? With *MANNY*?' And 'oh, you're late. Could you stay back today, then?' And 'oh, you're late. Do we need to change your starting time? *AGAIN*?' And 'oh, you're late. Are you going *MAD*?'

On the other hand, Camille's being late could create space for her and Holly to share an intimate moment together. Like, 'hey, Holly, I'm actually in pain, and I forgot my phone, which I appear to be addicted to, and my period's due, and do you know anything about that? Can you relate at all? To pain? To addiction? To menstruation? *To feeling?*'

Then maybe Holly would become super-empathetic and kind. Maybe she'd start to respect Camille, and to appreciate her input, and they'd finally be able to collaborate in a harmonious way. Maybe they'd start having long nights at the moody mahogany wine bar next door to Florals that Camille has always wanted to go to, and they'd share a dozen oysters with mignonette dressing, and they'd sip pinot grigio, because it has fewer calories and it goes down so easily, and they'd talk about ambition, and beauty, and power, and they'd reveal things about themselves, and they'd laugh, and everything would be amazing all of a sudden.

Now Camille is looking at the people inside Lord Byron — cutting into their poached eggs, sipping their freshly squeezed juices, checking their phones — and she wants to die of sorrow. Being in public, and eating in public, is so vulnerable. I mean, what the hell is everybody doing? Talking too fast? Not listening enough? Thinking about where they were yesterday? And where they hope to be tomorrow?

Camille wants to smash her head against that white brick wall with the Bromley portrait of some local socialite on it until she decapitates herself — because not having a head might give her space to think.

Two women in saris are walking past. They might be mother and daughter, because the woman walking in front is quite a bit younger than the woman walking behind. And the woman walking in front is wrapped in layers of green and silver, and the one at the back is swaddled in purple and trimmings of gold, and she has wisps of grey hair. They're both wearing bindis. And, thanks to the way Lord Byron's outdoor tables and chairs are positioned, Camille's knees grazed the older woman's sari as it wafted past her, and Camille smiled, and neither of the women smiled back. They just looked at her.

Whenever Camille sees people of faith, she feels hollow. She wants to be devoted to something bigger than her own mind. She wants to be a part of a community that believes in more than itself.

Years ago, she was walking down Lygon Street in Carlton on a hot and windy day. She was still at uni — 'paying to feel busy' as Manny would say. It was around 3pm, and close to forty degrees, and the road had that wobbly, greasy quality. The traffic was bad and Camille was weighing up when to cross the road. She kept looking back, and then looking up ahead, and that's when she saw The Woman in the Burqa. It was black and draped over everything except the woman's eyes. She was walking on the other side of the road and looking to cross it, too. But Camille could tell that she wasn't going to break her stride to do so.

The Woman in the Burqa briefly turned her head one way, and then the other, before stepping straight out onto the tar. Her gait was long and unapologetic. The burqa's fabric rushed forward and back around her body like a river. The material should've grazed the earth beneath her feet, but it didn't. Its length was of mystical proportions.

Then, all of a sudden, the street became deserted. The wind picked up, but it couldn't make the burqa flap, or flit about, like so many summer skirts and flimsy fabrics seem to do. And the woman didn't display an instinct to fiddle with it. She knew it would move.

And it did.

It's 9.59am, and Camille is rushing toward Florals with two coffees in hand. The lower part of her body is aching and she's hungry. She only had one bite of her avo toast. The roof of her mouth is dry. Her solar plexus is throbbing. And whenever Camille has a visceral physical experience like this, it's usually because whatever she's doing is a threat to her wellbeing. But rather than taking heed of this, she bargains with it. Like, 'ok, you did this to yourself by insisting on getting a coffee and then having to rush' and 'stop caring about what Holly thinks so much' and 'you don't have to get along with everybody, that's just not realistic' and 'you can be one minute late! *CHILL THE FUCK OUT*' and 'you learn so much from Holly. Maybe try some gratitude?' and 'just make sure to eat properly tomorrow' and 'Holly has connections that could help you down the track' and blah, blah, blah, none of it matters, because the body doesn't lie.

It knows.

And there's Holly.

Sitting in the little glass box she made.

There are two thirty-something women sitting opposite her donning some nice drip — asymmetrical tops, skirts, and boots. They must be from that exhibition space in Richmond. Or maybe that tech startup in Collingwood. They're both having openings in a week. That said, it's not a great day for Holly to have organised meetings? But Camille has a meeting, so. Maybe Holly organised her own meetings to spite Camille's meeting. And thanks to the presence of these women, Camille gets a couple of minutes to settle in before she has to deal with Holly's eyes, and Holly's words, and Holly's thoughts being directed at her, all at once. Coco is in the building, too. She gave Camille some side-eye as she popped Holly's coffee down, and Holly didn't acknowledge it. Camille's not even sure Holly is capable of genuine appreciation, anyway, so it's probably best not to expect anything. And Holly is laughing a lot. She has such a memorable laugh. It moves like a wave through everyone and everything around her. It's the kind of laugh that makes you want to laugh whenever you hear it.

Camille has snuck over to her corner of the space and lit her gardenia candle. She does love her corner of the space. Although, Holly doesn't love the fact that Camille loves her corner of the space. Nor that she's adorned it with framed photographs of flowers. Camille *did* ask Holly if it was ok to put the framed photographs up, and Holly wasn't really listening. She just shook her head, like, 'what? yes? ok? I'm busy and important? Who are you? Why are you asking unexpected questions of me? And surely you can see that I quite consciously caged you into the inferior desk space? And that your taking ownership of said desk space, and expressing yourself through it, is not what was intended? It was meant to crush you? Mmmmk ... ?' So Camille went ahead with framing the pictures, and putting them up, and about a month later Holly copied her. She acquired two enormous photographs of rare white waratah flowers, and she had them put in large gold rococo frames and delivered by truck to Florals, where they now hang over her seat, and her desk, as if she's sitting on a throne.

Prior to Camille's arrival at Florals, Holly was 110% pretending to be a minimalist, and Camille wanted to respect this. She figured no one would see her collection of flower pictures from outside the building when they were looking inside the building. Nor would they see them once they entered the building, unless they were encouraged to turn away from Holly and to look at Camille for a second, which was unlikely. And Camille receiving a compliment for the pictures — or for anything — was even less likely.

Whenever someone compliments Camille, she finds herself questioning what they're saying and refusing to believe it, because she doesn't think the human brain functions at its optimum in social situations. The context for the compliment is always off, because the stakes are too high. People want to fit in. They want to be liked. So it's, like, quick, say something. Anything. It's what's expected. It's what's custom. And it's happening now so *GRAB THE FIRST THING YOU CAN SEE*: 'oh, hey, I love your hat!' And 'oh, aren't you gorgeous!' And 'oh, wow, fab dress!' And 'oh, you look like you just walked off a red carpet!' And 'oh, aren't those piccies cute!' The adrenals get pumping, and the chin gets moving, and the meaning behind what's being said takes on less importance than the act of making noise. Kind of like when people are running from a predatory animal and blood flows to the parts of the body that need it most: legs, lungs, arms. In social situations, blood rushes to the mouth, and to the vocal cords, and Camille finds it hard to trust what comes out.

Holly just looked Camille up and down, and her escalator eyes didn't even reach Camille's face. They got to her neck and bailed. They had seen enough.

Camille can tell that, on some level, Holly would love it if she had the audacity to rock up to work in something other than black-on-black. Maybe Holly waits for that day. That sweet, sweet day when Camille dares to wear her favourite yellow Nirvana *In Utero* T-shirt and her baggy blue jeans. Then Holly will smile approvingly, before she casually mentions that Camille should consider wearing a warmer shade of yellow, perhaps, rather than a green-based one? And Camille will ask why, and Holly will say 'no reason', or she'll ignore the question. Or she'll be like, 'well, because yellow does suit you, *but* ...' and trail off. Or Holly will ask if the top belongs to Manny because, obviously, that would be what made it stylish in Camille's eyes, because she's a man-pleaser, and she can't think for herself. Or Holly will observe how 'boyfriend jeans' are very 'in' aren't they? Wearing them isn't an original idea of Camille's, because Camille isn't capable of original ideas. And Holly's been doing loose denim for, gosh, she doesn't even know *how* long? Lonnnngggg before it was a trend. Lonnnnggggg before the masses caught on. And was Camille even alive for Nirvana? Is she even old enough to be sufficiently educated in their musical repertoire? Is she even worthy of a piece of their *original* merchandise? When she wasn't even a member of their *original* audience?

Camille really wants to be one of those people that doesn't give a fuck about what someone like Holly thinks. One of those people would be so good at Camille's job. I mean, Camille has never actually met a person who genuinely didn't give a fuck about what others thought, even if she's met plenty of people who have *claimed* not to give a fuck about it. If anything, the people who have claimed not to give a fuck about what others thought have given more fucks than anyone else.

But everyone picks up on everyone else's unspoken juju, anyway, despite what they say, or do, or what they claim to be true for them. So Holly probably senses how much Camille cares about what she thinks, and all of Camille's torment about it, because Camille's not doing anything with it. Camille doesn't know how to channel her pain and to make it work for her.

One day she will. One day Camille's fury won't be aimed into a fluffy pillow, shrieking at itself wildly and hopelessly on the first day of her period. One day Camille is going to do something brilliant with it. Because fury is power. And when power is reclaimed, it's unstoppable.

Camille turned on her computer and the first email in her inbox was sent by Holly at 5.35am. Strange. Well, it's not strange to have an email from Holly. Holly prefers email communication to face-to-face communication, as she'd rather not have to be held accountable for the majority of her requests, because if the majority of her requests were put on some kind of trial, or exposed to even the most gentle line of questioning, they would quickly be deemed absurd and a waste of any living, breathing creature's time.

Yet via email Holly can inundate Camille with so many menial, ludicrous, life-sucking bits-and-bobs — and then feverishly chase Camille up about them — that Camille becomes discombobulated, and then when she mentions to Holly that she wants to work with clients more often, Holly will insinuate that Camille can't even handle the minor tasks she's assigned effectively, so how could she possibly be trusted with greater responsibilities? Because 'what's the schedule looking like for next winter again?' And 'have you made copies of all of our receipts even though we've never done that before?' And 'have the buckets in the warehouse been stacked?' And 'have you picked up the dry-cleaning?' And 'have you emailed updates about everything to me so as to keep me "in the loop" as I requested?'

Sometimes Holly will email Camille about random shit after hours — at say 7pm or 9pm — and Camille won't respond until she's at Florals. So Holly wouldn't necessarily expect a response to her 5.35am email by now. But a pre-10am email does raise some alarm. Camille's face feels hot with the knowledge that Holly's sitting there — laughing, glamouring — knowing exactly what this email is about. And Holly probably assumes that Camille has walked in here knowing exactly what it's about, too, because who doesn't have their phone on them at all times? And who doesn't check it at hourly intervals? At least? I mean, even if you don't reply, you've definitely *seen* the message dammit. *You've definitely seen it.*

The subject line is 'V Day'.

Hi Hun!!! I'm taking over the Mornington account! The girls need help with VDay orders & I need you to make sure the place is SPARKLING after :))))))))) so if you could you head out back that would be gr8!!! H xxxx

Camille is getting up, and walking through the building toward the warehouse, wondering when her life is going to start. Wondering when wondering is going to end.

Working with Tim and Eric symbolised the beginning of something. Something important. Something that means even more now that it's been taken away — and now that Camille's been relegated to Out Back. Out Back at Florals consists of the warehouse, the laneway, a small windowless corridor with a toilet, and a kitchenette, located behind Holly's and Camille's desks, which is demarcated by what is essentially a velvet vanity screen, erected with the sole intention of concealing Out Back from Florals' illustrious clientele. Nobody sees Out Back except for those working at Florals and the delivery drivers. Whenever clients ask to use the bathroom, Holly says there isn't one, and no one presses her on this.

Out Back there are two tiny doors. One leads to the toilet. The other leads to the warehouse. To the left of the toilet, there are three large filing cabinets. On top of the cabinets, there's a dark-blue feather duster, piles of loose papers, and manila folders. To the right of the door that leads to the warehouse, there's a white bench with a sink and a cheap plastic kettle sitting on top. There's a scary old microwave, a cupboard stuffed with old tea bags, and a series of Tupperware containers that no one uses.

Camille brings her own organic herbal tea bags to work. She keeps them in a jar on her desk. She's got licorice, fennel, and peppermint. Holly has never accepted a cup of tea from Camille or even a glass of water when Camille has offered her one. Holly is a camel. She prefers takeaway cups of coffee that serve a performative social purpose. But Georgia and Alyce *always* want Camille's teas, and this functions as a kind of secret code between the young women, a secret code that says: 'hey, we can't directly discuss how intense working here is, but we're all in this together, and we're all gettin' paid. Tea?'

An unplugged minibar fridge sits in the right-hand corner of Out Back and Holly doesn't want to pay for its electricity, so it pays tribute to the idea of refrigeration, and a certain degree of communal flow, and normalcy, without actually offering any. The flowers get more refrigeration than the people do.

Then there's dust, and darkness, and a lone fluorescent light stuck to the ceiling, which flickers whenever it's turned on. A navy handtowel lives beside the kitchen sink and, since Camille started working at Florals, it's never been replaced. There's also an unfortunate absence of cleaning products.

Camille bought some designer mandarin liquid soap around the corner on High Street, which she contributed to Out Back, but she couldn't bring herself to start a dialogue with Holly about the handtowel, because Holly never washes her hands after using the toilet. She walks straight back to her desk without a hint of self-consciousness. So to bring up the handtowel would open a door to a place Camille doesn't want to visit. Not for a day. Not for an hour. Not for a minute. There's no coming back from, 'ah, hey, Holls, I've noticed that you don't wash your hands, and that's probably why you're not motivated or inspired to change the handtowel because, yes, I see you, so I'll take over jurisdiction of the handtowel, and the cleanliness of your business, and the wellbeing of your staff, as you wither away in a strategically hidden cesspit of your own inconsiderate muck, and filth, which I pay witness to, and keep quiet as best I can on your behalf, ok?'

So when Camille got back from buying the designer mandarin liquid soap, she was like, 'oh, wow, smell this, Holly. Isn't it great? I bought it from that new shop next to the fancy macarons place. I couldn't resist! I'll just leave it here.'

Hi Hun!!! Hi Hun!!! Hi Hun!!! Hi Hun!!! Hi Hun!!! Hi Hun!!!
Hi Hun!!! Hi Hun!!! Hi Hun!!! Hi Hun!!! Hi Hun!!! Hi Hun!!!
Hi Hun!!! Hi Hun!!! Hi Hun!!! Hi Hun!!! Hi Hun!!! Hi Hun!!!
Hi Hun!!! Hi Hun!!! Hi Hun!!! Hi Hun!!! Hi Hun!!! Hi Hun!!!
Hi Hun!!! Hi Hun!!! Hi Hun!!! Hi Hun!!! Hi Hun!!! Hi Hun!!!
Hi Hun!!! Hi Hun!!! Hi Hun!!! Hi Hun!!! Hi Hun!!! Hi Hun!!!
Hi Hun!!! Hi Hun!!! Hi Hun!!! Hi Hun!!! Hi Hun!!! Hi Hun!!!
Hi Hun!!! Hi Hun!!! Hi Hun!!! Hi Hun!!! Hi Hun!!! Hi Hun!!!
Hi Hun!!! Hi Hun!!! Hi Hun!!! Hi Hun!!! Hi Hun!!! Hi Hun!!!
Hi Hun!!! Hi Hun!!! Hi Hun!!! Hi Hun!!! Hi Hun!!! Hi Hun!!!
Hi Hun!!! Hi Hun!!! Hi Hun!!! Hi Hun!!! Hi Hun!!! Hi Hun!!!
Hi Hun!!! Hi Hun!!! Hi Hun!!! Hi Hun!!! Hi Hun!!! Hi Hun!!!
Hi Hun!!! Hi Hun!!! Hi Hun!!! Hi Hun!!! Hi Hun!!! Hi Hun!!!
Hi Hun!!! Hi Hun!!! Hi Hun!!! Hi Hun!!! Hi Hun!!! Hi Hun!!!
Hi Hun!!! Hi Hun!!! Hi Hun!!! Hi Hun!!! Hi Hun!!! Hi Hun!!!
Hi Hun!!! Hi Hun!!! Hi Hun!!! Hi Hun!!! Hi Hun!!! Hi Hun!!!

Hi Hun!!! Hi Hun!!! Hi Hun!!! Hi Hun!!! Hi Hun!!! Hi Hun!!!
Hi Hun!!! Hi Hun!!! Hi Hun!!! Hi Hun!!! Hi Hun!!! Hi Hun!!!
Hi Hun!!! Hi Hun!!! Hi Hun!!! Hi Hun!!! Hi Hun!!! Hi Hun!!!
Hi Hun!!! Hi Hun!!! Hi Hun!!! Hi Hun!!! Hi Hun!!! Hi Hun!!!
Hi Hun!!! Hi Hun!!! Hi Hun!!! Hi Hun!!! Hi Hun!!! Hi Hun!!!
Hi Hun!!! Hi Hun!!! Hi Hun!!! Hi Hun!!! Hi Hun!!! Hi Hun!!!
Hi Hun!!! Hi Hun!!! Hi Hun!!! Hi Hun!!! Hi Hun!!! Hi Hun!!!
Hi Hun!!! Hi Hun!!! Hi Hun!!! Hi Hun!!! Hi Hun!!! Hi Hun!!!
Hi Hun!!! Hi Hun!!! Hi Hun!!! Hi Hun!!! Hi Hun!!! Hi Hun!!!
Hi Hun!!! Hi Hun!!! Hi Hun!!! Hi Hun!!! Hi Hun!!! Hi Hun!!!
Hi Hun!!! Hi Hun!!! Hi Hun!!! Hi Hun!!! Hi Hun!!! Hi Hun!!!
Hi Hun!!! Hi Hun!!! Hi Hun!!! Hi Hun!!! Hi Hun!!! Hi Hun!!!
Hi Hun!!! Hi Hun!!! Hi Hun!!! Hi Hun!!! Hi Hun!!! Hi Hun!!!
Hi Hun!!! Hi Hun!!! Hi Hun!!! Hi Hun!!! Hi Hun!!! Hi Hun!!!
Hi Hun!!! Hi Hun!!! Hi Hun!!! Hi Hun!!! Hi Hun!!! Hi Hun!!!
Hi Hun!!! Hi Hun!!! Hi Hun!!! Hi Hun!!! Hi Hun!!! Hi Hun!!!
Hi Hun!!! Hi Hun!!! Hi Hun!!! Hi Hun!!! Hi Hun!!! Hi Hun!!!
Hi Hun!!! Hi Hun!!! Hi Hun!!! Hi Hun!!! Hi Hun!!! Hi Hun!!!
Hi Hun!!! Hi Hun!!! Hi Hun!!! Hi Hun!!! Hi Hun!!! Hi Hun!!!
Hi Hun!!! Hi Hun!!! Hi Hun!!! Hi Hun!!! Hi Hun!!! Hi Hun!!!
Hi Hun!!! Hi Hun!!! Hi Hun!!! Hi Hun!!! Hi Hun!!! Hi Hun!!!
Hi Hun!!! Hi Hun!!! Hi Hun!!! Hi Hun!!! Hi Hun!!! Hi Hun!!!
Hi Hun!!! Hi Hun!!! Hi Hun!!! Hi Hun!!! Hi Hun!!! Hi Hun!!!
Hi Hun!!! Hi Hun!!! Hi Hun!!! Hi

Georgia and Alyce work at Florals three days a week. They watch over the stock and, before an event, they follow Holly and Camille's directions for constructing the arrangements. Then they carefully load the flowers, and the vases, and the arches, and whatever other props are required onto the trucks and into the cars. Sometimes when the arrangements are particularly complicated, they'll help to set them up at the venues. Essentially, Georgia and Alyce churn out the workload of about four full-time employees over the course of a few days, and with two sets of arms and legs.

Alyce always looks as if she's about to explode. She breathes quickly and her cheeks are perpetually flushed. She's short, soft, and round. People think she's younger than she is. She dons overalls and collects vintage dresses that she never wears. She's obsessed with Spanish cooking and she loves bringing fresh fruits and vegetables that she's grown into work: tomatoes, lemons, strawberries, potatoes. She's studying nutrition and her friends and family are all like, 'that's SO great.' And 'good for YOU.' And 'nice WORK.' As if studying nutrition is a way for Alyce to 'fix' herself, which it's not. She just adores food.

Then there's Georgia, and Georgia is obsessed with Camille. A while back, she started dressing like Camille, and Camille confronted her about this, because *Single White Female*, etc, and Camille would never subject herself to being caught copying someone IRL. The *indignity* of it. Camille prefers to quietly, and covertly, look to fashion magazines, celebrities, underground influencers, random people on the street that she'll never see again, foreign films, and 90s TV characters for style cues. She covers her tracks. But Georgia is a different beast. Georgia is shameless.

Georgia has a tiny, unassuming face, and an even tinier, unassuming apartment in North Melbourne with a single bed and a Russian housemate she never sees. Her capsule wardrobe includes every item she's noticed Camille wearing, plus a pair of thin-framed gold reading glasses. Then, when it got hot last year, she wore a woollen grey waistcoat with nothing underneath, because she saw a girl at Abbotsford Convent doing that one night.

'Morningggggg.'

'Hey, Camille.'

'Hiiiiiii.'

'Happy Valentine's Day!'

'Yeah, thank you. You too.'

'Is Manny making you a feast tonight?'

'I think so. We'll see.'

'So jealous. Such a vibe.'

'I brought heaps of lemons in if you need any? They're over there.'

'Always need lemons, Alyce. Thank you. How's it going in here? It already feels muggy.'

'Yeah, can we crank up the fans? Or will Holly crack it?'

'Just put them on. These look gorgeous.'

'Thanks, yeah! That change to the stem lengths really helped, I reckon.'

'Definitely.'

'So, we've peeled, like, one hundred roses, and dispatched three of the nine private deliveries for today. Like, the ones that specified that they needed to go before 10 or 11am. So kicking goals.'

'Nice.'

'And that order with the moss for the breakfast event in Kew has gone. So there's lots more space in the fridges now.'

'Excellent.'

'And the order with the peonies for that WAG's lunch is supposed to go next, but the driver isn't here yet. I tried to call him, but there was no answer. He's only five or ten minutes late right now, but. Yeah.'

'Have you told Holly?'

'What d'you think?'

'Fair enough. I'll go inside and call his supervisor. Anything else Holly hasn't dealt with?'

'Well, we couldn't find the display boxes for that order with the orchids later?'

'Oh?'

'Yeah, I swear they were on the shelves last Friday. Do you know where they are?'

'No idea, but I can ask Holly when I go inside.'

'Yeah, we were waiting for you. Neither of us wanted to go in there. She's been a bit *tetchy*.'

'All good. I get it. What time does that one need to go?'

'Umm ... 4pm. It must be for a dinner.'

'Oh, yeah, it's for that fashion mag's supper-club thing in the CBD.'

'He's here! The driver for the peonies is here!'

Camille waved to the driver on her way back to the office. He's wearing a bright-yellow high-vis T-shirt with a pen in the front pocket, and a black trucker cap, and his smile made her look away. No one gets enough credit for what they do.
No one.

'Morning, Holly.'

'Morning.'

'Do you happen to know where the display boxes are?'

'No? Which ones?'

'The ones that we're using for the orchids today.'

'Are they not in the warehouse?'

'No. Georgia and Alyce couldn't find them. They said they were on the shelves at the end of last week, but they're not there now.'

'Well, I have no idea?'

'That's strange.'

'That's what happens when it's a pigsty out there.'

'Yeah. I'll email the supplier and see if we can get a few more couriered over.'

'But will they get here in time?'

'The order doesn't go until 4pm. So. It should be ok.'

'Just make sure the girls don't rush the assembling process. It's obvious when they cut corners.'

'Yep, sure.'

'And Happy Valentine's Day.'

'Thanks. You too.'

'Has Manny spoiled you rotten?'

'Ah, I think we're just having a nice dinner.'

'You *think* you're just having a nice dinner?'

'Well, we are. It's what we always do.'

'But?'

'But nothing. I mean, we didn't really talk about it this morning or anything. It just kind of happens.'

'Hmm.'

'What?'

'Oh, nothing. You've just got a lot of faith in him. I would never trust a man with simply *knowing* how to celebrate

Valentine's Day. Are you kidding? Men have to be told. Although, not too directly, of course.'

'Oh dear.'

'Come on, Camille. You know what I'm talking about. Even if you don't want to admit it, you know what I mean.'

'Maybe.'

'And did you get my email?'

'Yes, thanks. I did.'

'Great, ok. So my plan for today is: you stay out back and help the girls, and deal with the display boxes, and everything. I'll go to LB in a bit. Then I'll keep working with the clients before you go and get lunch. Then I'll get you to wrap the girls up around 4pm and clean the warehouse.'

'I think Georgia and Alyce were expecting to work until at least 5 or 6pm today?'

'Were they.'

'Yeah, because it's busy, I guess? And our last pick-up is around 5pm, I think.'

'Well, could you please inform them that they won't be needed until then? The last two or three orders are small, so I was thinking that you could do them, and that you're more than capable of cleaning the place up after the girls finish at 4pm.'

'Ok.'

'Oh, and if you could grab Tim and Eric some coffees and treats from LB before they arrive, that'd be great. Don't you think that'd be great? To treat the clients? I think that's something we should start doing more often. Maybe I'll talk to Seamus about it.'

'We ... I ... don't know what coffees they drink?'

'Oh?'

'It'd be good if we could make them a coffee or a tea here?'

'Our kitchen isn't fit for that, hun. Maybe get some treats at LB. A few of those friands from the counter or something.'

'Ok.'

'And, just so we're clear, I'll get back from coffee, and then you can go and get the treats, and then Tim and Eric will arrive, and then you can keep helping with everything out back before you go and get lunch, like usual, and then send the girls home, and oversee those last orders, and do the big clean-up.'

'Yep, sure.'

Sometimes when an irrational person speaks or gives instructions they can sound rational, but something doesn't feel right. And then when you scratch beneath the surface of what they've said — when you have a millisecond to yourself between the onslaughts of their irrationality — the entire thing explodes in your face.

So Camille isn't going to ask Holly why the girls must knock off at 4pm, rather than 5pm or 6pm, because she knows why: Holly doesn't want to have to pay them. They're casuals and Camille is on a salary, i.e. she's the slave that can be overworked and exploited. This sleight of hand also ensures that Camille will be working and getting home to Manny later. Much later. Like, 9, 10, or 11pm later, depending upon which regional hourly train she manages to catch. *On Valentine's Day*. So. Is *this* Camille's punishment for refusing to come in over the weekend? Or before 10am? Is *this* a way to sabotage her time with Manny?

Camille wants to ask Holly why she isn't getting the treats for Tim and Eric herself when she goes down to LB in a minute, because Camille is going to be travelling back and forth between LB and Florals so many times today. And that technically isn't her job. Although, she's not even sure what her job technically *is* anymore. *DO WHATEVER HOLLY SAYS* sounds about right. Holly must be nervous about Camille intervening in proceedings with Tim and Eric, because Holly must've sensed how much fun the three of them had during their initial meetings, and Holly must've felt left out, so she now wants to exclude Camille from the fun times.

Camille is trying to find the email address of the supplier for the display boxes, and she's watching Holly pretend to do something on her phone before her next clients walk in, and Camille has become aware of herself overriding physical pain. Not only overriding physical pain, but feeling low-key proud of not showing how much physical pain she's in.

Camille is witnessing herself take some kind of sick pleasure in being a victim of Holly, and a victim of her body, and a victim of her circumstances, because it makes her feel alive, and alert, and a part of something. And, for a moment, she doesn't have to listen to Holly, or take anything Holly says or does as seriously, because Holly isn't the only noise in this place — there's something else screaming.

'Holly?'

'Mmm?'

'Maybe you could get the treats when you go down to LB in a minute?'

'It'd be easier if you went, hun. I have quite a bit to do here before the next clients arrive.'

'Oh, ok.'

'Do you have a problem with going down to LB?'

'No, no.'

'Because the treats will be fresher if you go down and get them just before Tim and Eric arrive.'

'Sure.'

Camille is hurting in her cold designer seat as she emails the supplier of the display boxes and wonders what Manny would say or do if he were in this situation. It occurs to her that he would most likely rip Holly a new one with his words, and with his intellect, and with his crystal-clear recollection of all the other occasions when Holly did something equally as nonsensical, and he'd elucidate upon these occasions, and the destructive pattern that can be identified from them, in vivid detail, right to Holly's face, driven by a shrewd sense of injustice and entitlement, and he'd be super impressive.

But Camille is too busy slapping herself in the face to be impressive or entitled. She's too busy 'getting on with it' and reminding herself that people are dying right now. People are being murdered. Raped. Drugged. Beaten. Starved. Poisoned. Operated on. Tortured. Resuscitated. Starved. Extracted from car crashes. Shit could be *SO MUCH WORSE* so she really should *GET OVER IT* because *BILLIONS OF PEOPLE* on this planet are doing jobs that they *HATE* right this instant. That's *LYF, MATE*. So *go on*. Go and organise the crazy lady's crap. Find her display boxes, and get her sugary treats, and clean up her mess, and get paid, and get over it. Who cares about *THE GAYS*? They didn't even *LIKE YOU* that much. You're *A MEANS* to an *END* for them. The *HELP. OCCASIONALLY. A SLAVE*, mostly. Whenever it suits *HOLLY*. Who is *YOUR BOSS*. At a job you have *CHOSEN TO DO*. So. Suck it *UP* and find a way to deal with *ALL OF THE RESENTMENT* 'cos *NO ONE WANTS TO HEAR IT* not even *YOU*.

Camille doesn't realise that the answer to all of this is quite simple, really. Quite banal, in the end. The answer is to say *no*. But, instead, Camille is imagining how she would explain all of this to a therapist. Or to a cop. Or to a judge. Or to a jury. It's so nuanced and ridiculous. It's so first-world. Manny gets it, because he's experienced the effect that working for Holly has had upon Camille across time. He's heard all of the bitching and moaning. He's absorbed all of the details. He's also met Holly once.

And that was memorable.

'That's Florals.'

'Ok.'

'Do you want to come in?'

'Not really.'

'Sorry, I meant to say "are you coming in?" because of course you don't *want* to come in. But are you coming in?'

'I don't know. Do you want me to come in?

'Yes. Well, I'm not sure. It depends.'

'On what?'

'You.'

'Would it be weird?'

'If you came in or if you didn't?'

'Either. Both.'

'Well ... ?'

'Does Holly know you're having breakfast with me?'

'No.'

'So I could sneak away?'

'Yes.'

'Fuck. No. I'll come in. Whatever. Is that her?'

'Of course that's her.'

'Shall we walk around the block first?'

'Really?'

'Ah ...'

'Morning, Holly. This is my boyfriend, Manny.'

'Oh!'

'Hi.'

'H-e-l-l-o. Gosh. Look what you've been keeping all to yourself, Camille.'

'Umm.'

'I'm sorry that Coco isn't in today! She would've *LOVED* to meet you.'

'Haha, yeah. Ok.'

'So what'd you do, Manny?'

'I ...'

'Is that short for Manuel?'

'Er, no. Manfred. Actually.'

'Manfred. Fantastic. And what brings you into the city, *Manfred*?'

'We, ah ...'

'Work with your hands?'

'Sort of?'

'Wait, let me guess. You're an artist. A painter. A sculptor. A ... gardener?'

'A poet, mainly. But. Umm. I fucking hate talking about it, so.'

'Don't you dare be modest. What're you doing in the city today, then? You didn't come all of this way just to meet *ME*, I hope?'

'We had breakfast.'

'At LB?'

'Umm?'

'Lord Byron.'

'Oh, yeah. We had breakfast at Lord Byron.'

'What did you have? Something substantial to fuel the rest of your day? I'll cover it.'

'What?'

'I'll reimburse you. My treat.'

'Really? Are you sure, Holly?'

'Stop it, Camille! Before I change my mind.'

'Oh, ok. Well. Thank you. That's very kind, Holly.'

'Don't mention it. Anyway, I'd better get back to work. Pleasure to meet you, Mister ... *Manfred*.'

And that
    was $55.20
    Camille never saw.

The next day, Holly wouldn't shut up about Manny. 'So how long have you two been together?' And 'but *why* did he come into the city?' And 'how've you trained him so well?' And 'what was his background again?' And 'what do his parents look like?' And 'what was his star sign?' And 'have you ever seen or met any of his exes? What were they like?' And 'so what is he? Six foot two?' And 'I hope you're keeping him on a short leash.'

Camille laughed and tried to brush it off, because she hardly ever questioned Manny's motives. She felt that she knew who he was intimately, as if he were an extension of herself. Even if Manny was a constantly evolving being, just like Camille, he wasn't a pariah. He wasn't a con man. There might be a fine line between being an artist and being a scammer, but Manny was no more a fraud than anyone else. But Holly's probing made it seem as if a woman could never know a man, never trust him, never bond with him. To her, a man was a vehicle to status and security. And it made Camille question herself and her relationship with Manny in a way that seemed undermining to them both.

'I don't know how you do it, Camille.'

'Do what?'

'Be with a man like Manny.'

'Why?'

'Do you ever check his phone?'

'No.'

'Such naivety.'

'Omg? Whatever.'

'Sorry, hun. But, look. Ok. So. He's at home writing "poetry" all day, is he?'

'Yes.'

'*Right*.'

'What do you think he's doing then, *Holly*?'

'I don't know, Camille. And neither do you, for sure. All I know is that you're the one working and putting yourself out there and he's the one at home in the country, alone, struggling with his "craft". To me, that seems like a breeding ground for disaster and *the oldest story ever told*. Ok? That's all I'm saying.'

In that moment, Camille felt relieved Holly had never added her to Florals' social media accounts.

Holly posts hundreds of pics of the work Camille, Georgia, and Alyce do, but she never mentions, tags, or acknowledges them. She'll tag suppliers, and influencers, and media outlets. But Coco gets more love and attention on Florals' socials than Holly's employees. And, now, Camille was glad. Because if Holly had been given the opportunity to see more of who Camille was, she would've fed off it like a vampire.

'You know, you don't look so good, Mill. Are you under the weather?'

'No. Just a bit tired maybe?'

'It's Monday! Go hard at the weekend?'

'Not really.'

'Take some ibuprofen?'

'Umm. No thank you. I'm good.'

'Aspirin?'

'No thanks.'

'When things gets bad enough, you'll want some. There are a few options in the kitchenette, I think? They're old, but. Oh, sorry. Incoming.'

And she's off. More clients. An older dude in a suit and a young person with a shaved head. Probably a not-for-profit.

A feeling of familiarity is washing over Camille. This isn't the first time Holly has organised lots of meetings on a hectic day so that she doesn't have to help in the warehouse or get caught up in too many communications with Camille. It's not the first time Holly has gone out of her way to maintain a frequency of busyness so as to avoid becoming too responsible for the machinations of her own business.

And it might be for the best. Because if Holly didn't have more clients right now, she'd probably be saying something to Camille along the lines of, 'look, Camille, you really should take the expired over-the-counter drugs I've offered you, because the way you choose to care for yourself clearly isn't working, because if it were, you'd function much like a robot, or maybe like a soldier, and there wouldn't be any ups-and-downs to your energy, and you would do what I said, when I said it, and you wouldn't have needs, and you wouldn't question things, and you wouldn't look under-the-weather, and you wouldn't use *flower essences,* and you wouldn't think, and you wouldn't feel, and you wouldn't make demands, and you wouldn't force me to reflect upon my own choices, so, given this, it's probably best you come around to my way of doing things, and the script I've written for your life, which happens to be a lot like the one I wrote for mine, but just different enough to ensure you don't excel as much as I have, so, here, come on, swallow this, down the hatch, shut the fuck up, you stupid bitch.'

Camille has spotted an email from Manny in her inbox. No subject. Contained therein is a gif from the film *Heathers*. Shannon Doherty's character is wearing a turquoise blazer and she's sitting next to a blonde character who is wearing yellow. They're in a school canteen and Shannen Doherty's character is saying 'I forgot' and it's written in big white letters across the bottom of the image.

Camille can't bring herself to reply to Manny yet. She can't figure out how to make a joke about it all. Manny is always ready to laugh about painful things, even as they're occurring. It won't seem like he's ready to laugh, but he is. He'll be mad, and ranting and raving, and if Camille has the courage to make fun of him, right then and there, the mood will soften, and he'll laugh, and she'll laugh, and the two of them will feel closer to each other.

Camille has tried to make fun of Holly when she's mad, and ranting and raving, and it's never gone well. Holly has then accused Camille of doing the exact same thing, or changed the subject, or stormed out of the room, or zoomed off in her Mercedes, or quickly criticised Camille for something totally unrelated like, 'well, what about _____ ? And when's the last time you _____? And where's the _____ ? And you may make fun of me, but the truth is that you _____ all the time.'

Holly won't soften after venting, either. Her tone only ever becomes more menacing, so as to create a climax and to have The Last Word, which she assumes Camille won't have the audacity to fight, and she assumes right, because Camille doesn't. And Holly's never apologised for anything. The Dothraki may not have a word for 'thank you', but Holly Hughes doesn't have a word for 'soz'. And she doesn't laugh at herself. Maybe that's the real test. If a person can laugh at themselves when they're at their worst, you can probably trust them. If not, you might have a problem.

Camille talked about Holly to a total stranger once to see what would happen.

    She met this girl at the sauna. Maybe Anna was her name? Camille found herself arriving at the sauna at the same time as Maybe Anna every Friday and eventually they started chatting. Maybe Anna was tall and skinny, with thin lips, and her energy was contained. When she started sweating more intensely in the sauna, she'd remain still. Camille would lean back against the wall, or cross her legs, or lie down. Most people would fidget, shuffle about, cough, loudly suck on their water bottles, rub their skin, or bail altogether at the five- or ten-minute mark. But not Maybe Anna. Maybe Anna was steadfast. And it turned out she'd worked in event managing. So when Maybe Anna asked Camille where she worked and Camille said Florals, Maybe Anna raised one of her thinly plucked eyebrows.

'And how do you find *that*?'

'It's fine. Yeah.'

'But how do you find working for Holly Hughes?'

'Oh. Holly's just Holly. She's passionate. She's a perfectionist. She has her own way of doing things. Sure, she has this kind of ... violent psychic quality. But I learn a lot from working under her.'

'Hmm.'

'Why?'

Maybe Anna took a long pause. Camille was struck by it, because she never feels confident enough to take pauses like that when she's in a conversation. Especially with someone she's just met. It made her wonder if Maybe Anna had dissolved into Sauna Brain Fog and was unable to respond. But her eyes were open.

Then Camille thought about an article she'd read that said Daniel Day-Lewis used to do the same thing when he was in press conferences for films he was promoting. Like, when he was being interviewed, he'd take heaps of time after being asked a question, and entire rooms filled with reporters from all over the world would sit, and wait, while he was *thinking*. Camille would love to be able to do that. To give herself space and time to think. The mere act of opening her mouth and breathing already feels like she's done, and said, too much.

'You know, you don't have to defend Holly or pretend she's

something that she's not to make yourself look better. You're not a failure because you're working for a psycho. We've all been there.'

'Ah, Holly?'

'Yes, Camille.'

'When you have a sec, could I grab that order form for the irises that are going out today? Just to double-check the numbers?'

'Here.'

'Thanks. Oh, and did you happen to add the number I said after I spoke to them on Friday?'

'What number?'

'Ah, the client called on Friday right before I left, and my computer was off so I asked you to change the number?'

'I don't remember that.'

'Right. Well. Maybe I'll call them to double-check.'

'Ok. I'm off to LB!'

'Ok.'

Coco just whimpered. Coco doesn't like being left alone in the office. Whenever Holly vacates the premises without Coco, which is often, the bitch will leap up from her cushion, and run to the glass, and sit there, and pant, and wait with her tongue out. She used to yelp, and swish her tail, and groan, and drool. She doesn't do that anymore. She just sits. Sometimes, if it isn't too hot or too cold, she'll lie down and press her body against the front window. Then, when people walk past and notice the window display, they'll smile and say, 'oh, look at that doggy in the window! How *gorgeous*!' And they'll remember Florals because of Coco.

Sometimes, Camille has sat with Coco and patted her, before trying to play with her in an attempt to coax her from her mournful stupor. Camille has cooed and jumped about, and Coco has been tempted to engage. Camille *knows* that she's been tempted, because Coco's looked out the window, and then back at Camille, and then back out the window, and then back at Camille. Instant gratification or future reward? Known or unknown? Then she'd pant a bit more before putting her head down and communicating, very clearly, that her duty was to the door and to awaiting Holly's return. Which was understandable, because Holly always fusses over Coco when she returns. It's one of the rare occasions when Camille gets to see Holly abandon her haughty demeanour. Initially, Camille wondered if Holly fussed about Coco as a kind of performance for those watching. Like, 'ooh, aren't I lovely? Look how nice and good I am with the planet's lesser beings!' But Holly can barely look at anyone after saying hello to Coco, and giving her a big rub, and a cuddle, as if this display of affection is too revealing. As if cuddling Coco says to onlookers, 'yes, I am capable of expressing tenderness and appreciation. Just not toward *you*.'

Holly would love it if Camille were more like Coco. In fact, everyone in Camille's life would probably love it if Camille were more like Coco. Come to think of it, Camille is already a lot like Coco. It's just that she's not a dog.

She's a human being.

Hopefully, Seamus will keep Holly entertained for at least half an hour down at LB. It is Valentine's Day, after all. So fingers crossed he'll pull out all the stops. Camille knows this is a lot to expect, but it wouldn't be the first time Holly has taken more than half an hour getting her performance-latte. Sometimes she's gone somewhere else altogether.

Holly would like to think that Camille doesn't notice this, but it's hard not to. Holly will disappear for hours at a time, and when she returns Camille doesn't feel comfortable asking her where she's been, because, usually, Holly is refusing to look at Camille, which either means she feels no obligation to inform Camille of her whereabouts, or she doesn't want Camille to *know* of her whereabouts. Either way, after these mysterious protracted absences, Holly's eyes, cheeks, forehead, and/or lips will be speckled with tiny bruises, or she'll be shiny and a bit swollen.

Eventually, Camille put two and two together. She came to

understand that Holly's forehead wasn't uncharacteristically smooth, and full, and largely unresponsive to heightened emotion because mother nature had singled her out, above all others, and decided to conceal her humanity.

Holly's been getting some man-made help with that.

Holly might rock the natural locks, and surround herself with flowers as if to say, 'hey, look at me, your favourite, liberated, grey-haired, super-fashionable, low-maintenance, kinda-famous flower-lover', but then she'll throw the phrase 'chronic expression' into a conversation, and Camille will choose not to query it, or to engage Holly in a deeper discussion about it, because it wouldn't really be a discussion. To Holly, nobody under the age of fifty could ever contribute to a discussion regarding the appearance of the body or the face after fifty — because that's under the jurisdiction of those over fifty wishing that they weren't.

Camille finds it difficult to comprehend why anyone reveres youth. To Camille, young people suck. Young people are soft and easily manipulated putty. She really can't fathom why they're looked upon as beacons of beauty and wisdom. Or why every form of media she consumes seems to be frothing over what the latest hot young influencer/musician/designer/model/novelist/actor/activist/entrepreneur is up to. Or why they're being asked questions that would be fascinating to hear answered by someone older. Because at twenty or thirty, people have just learned to speak.

Yet Camille is bombarded by pimply, awkward tweens who are being showered with attention and admiration, and asked questions like, 'so, what last gave you pause for reflection?' and 'what do you see when you look in the mirror?' and 'what's the best piece of advice you've ever been given?' The irony being, of course, that Camille is young. But she already feels past it.

In recent years, she's developed a deep vertical line between her eyebrows. It's about an inch long. She notices it in photos, and she catches glimpses of it in the bathroom mirror, and in shop-window reflections. In certain lighting, it can't be seen, but then, at particular angles, it's practically startling. A while ago, she tried taking zinc and vitamin A supplements, and she seriously thought The Line was disappearing. But it wasn't. So now she wonders about it. Like, what does it mean? Is it some form of punishment? Does she need to detox her liver? Again? Is it genetic? Or is she simply a hopeless 'chronic expressor'? Doomed to experience the same emotions over and over again for eternity?

Camille studies people's faces to see if they have The Line, too. She furrows her brow to find all of the other furrowed brows and, as far as she can tell, most people develop two lines between their eyebrows, not one. But Michael Jordan has The Line. Adam Goodes, the ex-AFL player, has it, too. Then there's that guy from Harry Potter with the deep voice who died a few years ago. He had it. Princess Diana had it. Gillian Anderson from *The X-Files* has it, but she's the only living woman Camille can find that does, and it's nice to see, and it's nice to know, because a lot of women try to hide that kind of thing behind fringes, and foundations, and concealers, and hats, and injectables, and surgeries, because they're inundated with terms like 'chronic expression' and they feel out of place in the body they belong to.

Camille wishes that she could be like, 'you do you, Holly,' but she can't. Camille looks at Holly and she feels angry and frightened. It is only time between them, after all. So Camille worries about all of the lines and all of the saggy skin that is to come. She frets about how she's going to deal with it if she can't even handle The Line. She becomes tense thinking about all of the money she could justify spending in the process of fighting herself. Fighting nature. Fighting God.

Then she thinks about all of the women who wore corsets Once Upon a Time — and Camille doesn't look down upon them. She doesn't judge them for their corsetry. They were doing what they believed they had to do in order to fit in and to be desirable, even if it meant broken ribs, and shallow breath, and no food, and fainting, and bruising. She probably would've done the same.

Then Camille walks past all those pearly-white beauty salons throughout Armadale promoting lasers, and fillers, and chemical peels, and four different kinds of Botox, and she can't help but be tempted. They make it look so easy and inviting. Then Camille thinks about Manny. She's too scared to discuss any of this with him, because bringing up something like The Line would make it too real. And maybe it would draw his attention to her humanness, and to her flaws, and it might negatively impact whatever ideal he has of her — and whatever ideal she has of herself.

Then Camille fantasises about going into one of those salons and having The Line filled right up and seeing what happens. If it hurts. If it helps. If it's expensive. If it's invasive. If it's actually no big deal. 'It'll dissolve in a few months' and 'I don't have to get it done again if I don't want to.' Then Camille feels relieved for having given herself permission to fill The Line and less inclined to do anything about it.

Camille really wants to look in the mirror and to love what she sees through every phase of her life, but she fears that her body and face are going to define her. Then she tries to forget about it, because surely stressing about her appearance is going to create the very lines and saggy skin that she dreads. It's a vicious cycle; a cycle that Camille really wants to break by loving herself. It's just that she spends so much time hating herself. On some level, she must be addicted to hate. Because it lives in her.

And she's scared of it.

A little while ago, Camille had this rage blackout thing. It was as if the part of Camille that wants to punish and destroy her took over every cell and fibre of her being. It started shrieking and it struggled to stop. It popped tiny blood vessels around her eyelids, and under her eyes, and across her neck. There was one tiny blood vessel that didn't immediately heal under her right eye, and she fretted that it was never going to. Manny said it would, but Camille seriously thought it might be there until she left her body. But it disappeared after a week, and then she forgot about it.

Camille thought she'd lost everything on her laptop. She'd dutifully 'updated' the thing when it told her to do so. Then Manny told her that she needed to fix her privacy settings after the update, and Camille told *him* that she couldn't be bothered. So he gallantly went to do it for her, and something happened with the cloud, and all of her files and images vanished. They weren't even in the trash. All of

Camille's carefully laid-out and colour-coded thoughts. All of her recipes for different flower-essence blends and fragrances. All of her projections for starting her own business. All of her saved images of properties in rural New South Wales, and different floral arrangements, and hand-blown glass vases that could be bought in bulk. All of the details of graphic designers that might be able to create the look of her business. All of it had been erased.

Camille thought one yelp would release the agony, but the yelp turned into a shriek, and the shriek turned into tears, and the tears turned into heartbreak.

She kept having flashes of when she was at a friend's eighth birthday party in this Italian restaurant. She went to use the bathroom, and while she was in there, the lights got turned off, and Camille found herself stuck in pitch-black darkness. She couldn't see her body. No hands, no legs, no tummy. She could hear the party. The music. The laughter. The running around. But the sense of distance between the known and the unknown kept widening. Then Camille started yelling, and yelling, until the birthday girl's grandma threw open the door, and artificial light flooded in, and the older woman looked down at Camille. 'Well. You've got *quite* the pair of lungs on you, young lady.'

Fast-forward twenty years, and Camille is scared that the cops are going to rock up because the neighbours have called about a domestic disturbance. But Camille can't be thrown into the divvy van for shrieking, can she? Because it complicates things when the violence is inside her, doesn't it? When she is the abuser and the abused? The screamer and the screamed?

After a while, Camille's shrieking died down, and her hands stuck to her face. They covered her eyes, and her nose, and her mouth. Breathing into her palms was stabilising. Warm. Sweet smelling. Cushiony flesh against her nostrils

one day she won't have hands

one day she won't have skin

one day she won't be able to make a sound

one day she won't be able to breathe

one day she'll be gone

no one knows where

Then Camille noticed that her laptop was gone, and that the room was dark, and that the lights in the lounge were on. So she peeled herself off the floor, and plodded in there, and Manny was sitting and reading a book of Peter Schjeldahl essays with a tea. Camille's laptop was on the coffee table in front of him. She sat down and rested her head on his shoulder.

'It's fixed.'

'Everything's back?'

'Everything's back.'

'Oh my god.'

'Yeah.'

'Thank you.'

'It's ok.'

'And I'm sorry.'

'Yeah. Me too.'

Last year, Camille made a cake for Manny's birthday (May 24, *The Day of the Magnifier*). It was a double-tiered dark-chocolate cake with raw cacao powder, mashed banana, coconut yoghurt, almond meal, potato starch, vanilla essence, and cinnamon. She added shatavari drops and some rose essence she'd distilled from flowers in the garden. She made a ganache frosting to cover the top, middle, and sides, which was composed of dates, cashew butter, oat milk, and cacao. Finally, she whipped up some coconut cream to go on the side.

Then, on the day, she spread the ganache over the pre-made layers of cake, and she licked the spatula, and she adorned what was becoming quite a multilayered spectacle with fresh raspberries, goji berries, small gold candles, and sparklers. It was just her and Manny celebrating, which meant they could eat cake for days. Breakfast, lunch, and dinner. Happy Birthday *to you*.

Camille served sweet wine as an accompaniment — an

Australian one, with a fancy gold font, and lots of stickers and awards — and she sang 'Happy Birthday', and she kissed her beloved Manfred, and she sat back in her chair, and she watched him take a bite and hum with delight, before she sank a fork into the cake that had sprung from her heart, and she tasted its sweetness, and its naturalness, and its richness, and she felt all of the feelings, and it became apparent that this was a cake of power. This was a cake of Camille's. And it wasn't just for Manny. It was for her, too.

27

Camille spends a lot of time considering what it means to be an empowered woman. She'd really like to be one. She just can't imagine the empowered version of herself. Sometimes she feels her when she touches Manny. Sometimes she senses her when she's working with flowers. But, most of the time, it's when Camille is wanting what she doesn't have that she feels the closest to who she's meant to be. Then she feels held hostage by her dreams and she wonders if, maybe, it'd be better if she didn't dream.

One overcast and cold weekend, Camille binge-watched an entire season of this TV show, and every time the main character ended up in bed with a guy, or she made progress at work, it was by 'accident'. Apparently, the protagonist had no real dreams or aspirations of her own. Just 'good intentions'. She had an older woman for a boss, and her boss was super sassy, and Manny came in at one point, and was like, 'check it out. It's you and Holly.' The show was intended to be a fantasy: a high-definition exercise in product placement, broad stereotypes, colour, and movement. But it deeply disturbed Camille, because it seemed to suggest that the only way a woman can get what she wants is if she pretends not to want it.

The lead girlwoman was always like, 'oops! Sorry!? I knocked on the wrong door and I didn't realise I had a hot neighbour?!' And 'oops! Sorry!? I didn't mean for the CEO to fall in love with me, and to start buying me lingerie, and perfume, and to make these big business deals with the marketing firm I started working for!?' And 'oops!? Sorry! I didn't realise you were involved with him?!' And 'oops!? Sorry! I didn't even *want* or seriously think I'd *get* that other job I was going for in secret?!' And 'oops!? Sorry! But I'm going to insist on making you and the whole world better even though I don't know what my own values are!?' And 'oops! Sorry!? I actually *do* go for the occasional midriff-exposing jog, which centres around my taking selfies in front of photogenic landmarks that make me look like a connoisseur of things when I'm not, because, oops! sorry?! I'm not actually interested in culture, or in history, or in the outdoors, or in how my body feels, or in the power of having a physical outlet, or in the benefits of spending quality time with myself, or in the inexplicable force that is being alive?! 'Cos *OOPS SORRY I'M ALWAYS APOLOGISING AND ACTING LIKE A VICTIM AND BEHAVING AS IF I DON'T KNOW WHAT I'M DOING BECAUSE THEN YOU WON'T BE SCARED OF ME OR HORRIFIED BY MY ACTIONS WHEN YOU REALLY SHOULD BE 'COS I'M PRETENDING TO BE SOMEONE THAT I'M NOT 'COS I'M QUITE SURE THAT OVER TIME YOU'LL BECOME DESENSITISED TO THIS AND YOU'LL CONVINCE YOURSELF THAT I'M ACTUALLY HARMLESS AND*

VULNERABLE AND SWEEEEEEET WHEN I'M NOT 'COS IT'S ALL A GAME TO MAKE YOU QUESTION YOUR INSTINCTS AND TO MISTRUST THOSE WHO TRULY SPEAK THEIR MINDS AND FEEL THEIR FEELINGS AND EXPRESS THEIR THOUGHTS AND CREATE THEIR CREATIONS AND TAKE RISKS 'COS YEAH THOSE PEEPS ARE REALLY JUST SUPER PARTICULAR AND CRAZY AND DIFFICULT AND SELFISH AND ARROGANT AND LEWD AND STUFF SO LISTEN TO ME LOOK AT ME 10 9 8 7 6 5 4 3 2 1 YOU'RE NOW GOING TO WANT TO BE ME AND YOU'RE NOT EVEN GOING TO KNOW WHY ALL YOU'RE GOING TO REMEMBER IS THE IMAGE OF ME SMILING AND SHRUGGING AS MY LUSTROUS LOCKS BOUNCE AROUND MY BONY BARE SHOULDERS AS I HOP ACROSS THE COBBLESTONES IN STILETTOS CARRYING A CLUTCH IN THE CROOK OF MY ARM AND A GIANT PHONE IN MY GLOVED HAND WEARING A PINK BUCKET HAT THAT YOU'RE GOING TO WANT TO BUY 'COS I'M ACCIDENTALLY EVERYTHING AND IF YOU'RE NOT YOU'RE NOTHING

During winter last year, Holly and Camille had a fight.

It was a dark, dank Melbourne afternoon. Camille was at her desk sipping a peppermint tea and reading about a floral designer in the States who uses lots of unlikely foliage in her work. She includes seaweed, and mushroom plants, and tomato flowers, and olive branches, and seasonal fruits. Nothing is off limits. Her designs embrace everything the earth has to offer. And the shapes that this creates, and the shadows, and the multitude of textures, and layers, and unusual details, and curls, and edges, and openings, were hypnotic. It was easy for Camille to get lost in the possibilities. And Georgia was really into it, too. Alyce was trying to look busy fiddling with the golden wattle in the window display, and Holly was huffing and puffing at her desk.

'What are you two doing?'

'Ah. We're reading about this Malibu-based floral designer who uses lots of unexpected plants in her work. Do you want to see?'

'Isn't there something else you could be doing?'

'I'm not sure. Things seem slow today?'

'Do they.'

'Yes.'

'I'm sorry, I wasn't aware that you were the one determining our expectations and workloads, Camille?'

'Sorry, Holly. It's not that there's nothing to do. It's just that you haven't given us anything to do. Like, you're doing it all.'

'Ok, but I, *like*, hired you all to think for yourselves and to work. Not to be minions that I have to order around all day.'

'Well, technically, what we're looking at could help the business.'

'Could it.'

'Yes.'

'Camille. Sitting around and staring at women on the other side of the world who are more successful than you doesn't count as a positive contribution to this business.'

'We're not sitting around staring at women who are more successful than *us*, Holly.'

'Oh, no?'

'No. We're sitting around staring at women who are more successful than *you*.'

Sometimes, Camille worries that she'll have to become a tyrant in order to overcome tyranny.

'Omg, I'm so sure there were meant to be twelve of those irises? I'm tripping out.'

'Ten.'

'Are you sure?'

'That's what it says on the order form, isn't it?'

'Yeah. It's just that I spoke to them on the phone last week and I could've sworn they said twelve. I told Holly the number, but she doesn't remember. Gah! I should probably call and double-check? But I guess they need to go now.'

'Are you ok, Camille? You look a bit clammy.'

'I'm ok. I think? I mean, I didn't have enough breakfast.

And I forgot my phone. And I've got period pain. And it's Valentine's Day. So. You know how it is.'

'I do, babe. I do. And you forgot your phone? Jesus.'

'Yeah.'

'I don't know what I'd do without my phone.'

'I know, right. Phones aren't just phones. They're definitely, like ... *something else*.'

'Totally. And I guess there's nothing I can do to help with that, is there?'

'No. It's definitely a Me Problem.'

'I could make you a tea with some of the lemons I brought in? But I guess it's pretty hot, though, and we don't have any ice ...'

'Thanks, Alyce. It's ok. I'll be alright. Maybe I'll go inside and try to give these people a call about the irises.'

'Oh, did you ask Holly about the display boxes?'

'Yeah, she said she didn't know anything about them, so I've ordered more. They should be here any minute.'

'Cool, yeah, because we really need to get moving on that one.'

'True. I'll go and check where the courier is. Anything else?'

'Nah, all good!'

Holly has returned from whencesoever she may have been, and she's holding a single red rose, and she's trying not to make a big thing about it, but she keeps smelling it. So she *is* making a big thing about it, but in a way that would appear as if she's not making a big thing about it, because she wants *Camille* to make a big thing about it, and to be like, 'hey, what's that, Holly?' But Camille rarely takes the bait in these kind of situations. Instead, she pretends that she can't sense what's going on, and then she feels like a wretched person. Suffice to say, things must have gone well down at LB. But it's past midday. Tim and Eric are due at 1pm. Holly's cutting it fine. She could've got the friands herself. And the latte Camille bought her is still sitting on her desk. The foam on it has gone flat.

'Apparently, the courier with the display boxes should be here any minute. And I guess I'd better get down to LB.'

'Yes, great, ok! Thanks, hun. And when you get back, maybe pop the treats on a plate or something. Do we still have one of those white ones out back?'

'I'll check.'

'Oh, and do we still have that little milk-bottle vase?'

'Ah, yep.'

'Could you pop some water in it and bring it here?'

'Sure, yeah.'

'Not too much water, though.'

'I know. Here.'

'Thanks. Pretty, isn't it?'

'It is.'

'Seamus gave it to me.'

'Did he.'

'Oh, you're so cynical, Camille. Where's the romantic in you? Your partner is a poet! I don't know how he survives.'

'Me neither.'

'Anyway, you lay out those treats when you get back from

LB and then keep helping the girls. Easy-peasy. Then they can knock off.'

'At 4pm, right?'

'Yes. That's what I said.'

It must've rained again. The pavement is steaming and it has that moist cement smell. There are more people in the shops and walking to and from Armadale station. Camille isn't usually in and out of Florals so much during the day. It's a bit dizzying. But it gives her a break from Holly. And Lord Byron seems pretty chill now. There are a few people sitting out the front. Two guys are perched in a patch of sun with an English bulldog lying under their table and they've got Bloody Marys.

'Camille! Camille!?'

'We thought it was you!'

'Come join us?!''

'Hello! Ok. Well ...'

'Happy Valentine's, babe.'

'Thanks. You too.'

'Racked up any Valentines?'

'Only one, and I'm not sure I racked him up, exactly. I kind of ... scooped him up. He's at home.'

'Brilliant.'

'To be honest, we were starting to worry that we'd be late to Florals.'

'Yeah, and we were just talking about that native you threw into the mix during our last meeting. The empress-y one?'

'*Epacris impressa.*'

'*YESSSS.*'

'Pink common heath. It's the emblem of Victoria.'

'Omg, we're so happy with that one, babe. Seriously. It's changed our whole vibe for the day. Now when we imagine the winery, and the sunset, those drape-y luscious buds are a central feature. We're actually thinking that we'd like the whole thing to be natives.'

'Ohhh.'

'Yeah! It makes so much sense to use flowers that come from the *actual* region. Like, I can't believe we didn't think of that before?'

'No worries. No worries at all. And you know — I'm not sure — but I think Holly is taking over today. So your next phase of planning is going to be with her.'

'Oh?'

'Yeah. Although, I do need to go in and order a few things.'

'But then come back and sit!'

'Ok! One sec.'

Camille is standing at the counter and there are no friands. Only muffins. She can see Tim and Eric through the front window. Tim is wearing small round glasses with coloured lenses, which soften the intensity of his gaze — a fashionable way to seem less threatening. Eric keeps checking his phone, and mindlessly lifting his Bloody Mary, and taking a sip from it through LB's signature yellow-and-white striped straw.

Their food has arrived — Tim's having eggs Florentine with extra spinach, and Eric's having a mountain of scrambled eggs on sourdough with smoked salmon. Seamus is cracking fresh pepper over the top of their meals with a big red wooden pepper grinder, and the two men are grinning at each other.

'Hey, friend. Another coffee?'

'Yeah, thanks.'

'Soy cap?'

'Yes. And three skinny lattes. And three of those muffins. And maybe put the coffees from earlier on the card, too.'

Camille is ravenous, but she can't bring herself to deal with that. Having to explain to Holly why she put a meal on the business card is too much. And the fact that Tim and Eric want to use natives now is too much. Too much, too much, too much. Holly is going to hate that.

Camille could've taken the new direction with the *Epacris impressa* and run with it. She could've kept the natives soft and sumptuous, and made sure to add some *Boronia megastigma* or 'heaven scent'. But now she has to hand the whole thing over to Holly, who will either find a way to charge the men more for their use of natives or manage to talk them out of the natives altogether, because she has an almost superhuman capacity to be able to do that.

The synapses in Camille's brain are slowing. Period Brain is setting in. She's walking back outside with the muffins, and she's sitting down with Tim and Eric while she waits for her second coffee, and all of the other coffees. Coffees, coffees, coffees. They've introduced her to Travis, who is lying under the table, and who has taken it upon himself to move his head over and onto Camille's feet. Sweat is seeping into the linen crushed between Camille's thighs, and onto the white plastic chair, and she's squinting in the glare of the February day, and hearing about how Tim proposed to Eric in the shower. She's being shown photos of their new home in Clifton Hill, and the marble redo of the bathroom that's underway, and the veggie garden. Rocket is their favourite thing to grow.

'It goes on e-v-e-r-y-t-h-i-n-g.'

Seamus has sauntered over and asked Camille if she wants a glass of water. She said no, but Eric and Tim lit up at the sight of him, and cooed, 'oh, yeah, go get her one.' Before making a series of 'tall glass of water' jokes.

Eric and Tim met at Meredith Music Festival. Their partners at the time knew each other, and they were all moshing it to Grimes: glitter dust and beer flying everywhere.

Eric looked at Tim, and Tim looked at Eric, and they knew they had a problem

a love problem

a destiny problem

a twin flames problem

Fast-forward two years, and they're engaged, and living a life of domestic bliss. During Camille's first meeting with them, she noticed how invested they both were in the process of creating the floral arrangements, and it moved her. Maybe it's because they work in fashion and art. It's just rare to have both partners so motivated about the floral design of their event — usually one person is more into it than the other.

Tim and Eric's plates are empty, and Camille's coffee is finished. She's buzzing. Everything is tingly. Talking is continuing. Time is passing. Lots of time. Liquid time. Camille doesn't know how much time or what the time is because

she

doesn't

have

her

phone

and she can't see a clock anywhere

Eric's smart watch keeps slipping under his sleeve

and the screen is hard to see in direct sunlight

it must be *well* after 1pm

'So, do we even need to go to Florals? Maybe we can order more food and drink and do the rest of the meeting here? Then have ... *DESSERT*.'

'Oooh, yes.'

'Ah, I have a feeling that Holly would love to see you both. Umm. That sounds weird! She's not your mum. But. Ah. There are mock-ups at the office and some references on the computer. So?'

'No worries. I'll get the bill.'

Camille, Tim, Eric, and Travis are now walking across the bridge that joins the Lord Byron side of Armadale Station to the Florals side of Armadale Station, and Camille is trying to pre-empt what to say and do when they get to Florals, while maintaining conversation, and admiring Travis's muscly dog-body as it ripples and shines and proudly trots alongside his masters.

So Camille is smiling, and laughing, and planning, and sweating. She can't feel her legs. She really needs to eat. She really needs to ground herself. But to a passer-by she would seem fine. Even to Tim and Eric she would seem fine. Camille can seem very 'fine' when she wants to. Come to think of it, upholding 'fineness' has been Camille's job for the past three years. Not unlike the job of a domestic violence victim who must plan for and defend the behaviour of an abusive spouse. Like, 'oh, it's fine, they're just super sensitive about being left out,' and 'oh, it's fine, they just get worked up when they've had a bad day,' and 'oh, it's fine, everything will go smoothly as long as they're the centre of attention,' and 'oh, it's fine, they've just had a bit too much to drink,' and 'oh, it's fine, things are just trickier when their team has lost,' and 'oh, it's fine, they just wanted something to go a certain way and it didn't,' and 'oh, it's fine, if I frame what I have to say really carefully, and if I self-censor a bit, everything will work out,' and 'oh, it's fine if I just *act* like everything is fine'.

Camille is having flashes of occasions when she wasn't even *thinking* about Florals or about Holly. Like the time she, Manny, Lola, and Pope drove to the coast. It was a sweltering afternoon in January. Thirty-six degrees. They arrived at their rental property and decided to leave the dogs inside with tons of drinking water and go down to the beach, because the only place to be was in the sea.

Manny and Camille walked at the water's edge for what felt like miles before they picked a spot to put down their towels. Nobody could be seen in the distance and nobody walked past. Initially, Camille had her bathing suit on, but as the day wore on, it came off. She didn't think of her phone, which was back at their accommodation. Manny had brought his phone to the beach 'just in case', but then he'd left it in the glove box of the car, and he'd only realised once they'd traversed the sand dunes, and he couldn't be bothered going back to get it.

Camille didn't think of Holly or of anything, really. She thought about the heat and about ensuring that she didn't drift out too far while floating. She'd brought a thermos of filtered water with ice and slices of cucumber, and she had to keep moving it around as the sun moved. Then she'd run up the sand dunes, and take a sip, and the cold would drip down her chin, and onto her chest, and everything beyond the beach seemed absurd. Because waves crash. Sun hot. Water wet. Flies fly. Sky endless. Where is lack? Where is urgency? Where do they even come from?

'We really need to live near a beach.'

'I know.'

'It'd probably good during bushfire season, too.'

'I know.'

'And just good, you know?'

'I know.'

Manny went to his towel and grabbed his camera. He took a picture of Camille lying naked in the shallows. She didn't change her position, or look in a different direction, or think about what angle he might be capturing. Then it registered to her that the photo might suck. Manny might get it developed, and when Camille sees it, she'll think her naked body looks horrific, and then the day will be ruined for time immemorial. No wonder some First Nations people refuse to have their pictures taken. Some of them believe it's bad luck to see images of the dead, because you're supposed to let them go. You're supposed to let everything go. Living is letting go.

Camille sank back into the sand and her limbs became buried by the heavy wet. Then a bright-pink evening began streaking itself across the horizon, and Camille understood, perhaps for the first time, that a sunset really can tell you everything you need to know.

'Camille, I tried to call you?'

'Yeah, so ...'

'Oh!'

'Hello!'

'Hi there!'

'I don't have my phone, sorry.'

'We kidnapped your girl. We were having brunch and, *hello*. Who is this beautiful creature?'

'Coco! This is Coco.'

'Hey, Coco. Meet Travis.'

'Isn't he gorgeous! Oh, Coco loves bulldogs.'

'Oops! Sorry.'

'She'll calm down in a minute.'

'Ah, Camille?'

'What's up, Georgia?'

'Yeah, hey. Sorry to interrupt, but umm. The display boxes haven't arrived.'

'What?'

'Yeah. We weren't sure what to do.'

'So shall we park over here, Camille? Or?'

'Actually, it's probably best if you two come and sit at my desk. Camille's is a mess, and I've got everything set up here.'

'Oh, ok?'

'In fact, Camille has some work to do out back now. It's crazy in here — Valentine's Day and all! — so I thought I'd help you. And this is Georgia. She'll be assisting with construction when the time comes.'

'Hi.'

'Hey!'

'Hello.'

'Ok?'

'Well, I guess I'll head out back. Here are your coffees. And muffins.'

'Were those for us?'

'Ah, yeah. Sorry. I guess I should've given them to you already. Sorry.'

'Ok, thank you, Camille. And is there anything specific I need to be aware of that you discussed over brunch with these lovely gentlemen?'

'Well, they're really happy with the pink common heath as a central feature.'

'Yes, we're *loving* that. Such a great addition.'

'Lovely. But that was discussed at the last meeting, yes?'

'Umm. Yes. Yes it was.'

'So no further progress was made over brunch?"

'Actually, they're thinking of just using natives now.'

'Ah? I see.'

'Yes! We're very excited about that.'

'Interesting. Ok, then. Let's get down to business! Oh, and does Travis need some water, Tim?'

'Yes! Actually. That'd be great.'

'Perfect. Camille, hun, could you top up the dog water bowl?'

'What time is it?'

'Three-ish.'

'Shit.'

'Can I help with anything?'

'No, it's ok. I'll call the supplier. I'm so sorry. Is Alyce still in the warehouse?'

'Yeah, we've been trying to do as much prep as we can without the boxes. And I think that order with the irises *was* for twelve, not ten. The driver called and said the client was unhappy. That they'd spoken to you.'

'Omg. Ok. I guess there's nothing we can do about that

now. There are some irises left over, right? Umm. No, no, I'll call the supplier about the display boxes before dealing with that — oh, fuck. I don't have my phone.'

'You can use mine?'

'Thanks.'

'You're sweating?'

'Yeah, I think the second coffee I had spun me out.'

'Oh no! I probably need to get back to Alyce, but I could make you a tea or something first?'

'No, no. It's fine. Thank you. I'll just make this call.'

Every time Holly laughs with Tim and Eric on the other side of the vanity screen, Camille feels like she's being stabbed. Then she berates herself for being a baby, before she tries to block it all out, and to focus on what she's doing. Then she remembers the physical pain that she's in, and that she's hungry and light-headed, and that she wants to scream, before she stares at the invoices in her hands until they scatter into blurry black numbers, and words, because none of it means anything.

'Hi! It's Camille from Florals. I was just wondering where the courier is with the order of display boxes for today? They were meant to be here hours ago.'

The display boxes are en route from Richmond. Fifteen

minutes. Twenty max. That'll give Georgia and Alyce — who Holly wanted to be heading home — half an hour to assemble the entire order before they're supposed to be picked up and delivered to the CBD. And now it sounds like Tim, Eric, and Travis might be leaving.

'Can you come in here, Camille?'

'Coming.'

'They're fabulous, aren't they?'

'Yeah.'

'You were doing fine, alright? It's just that there were other things that needed attending to. And brunching with the clients isn't really your job, you know?'

'Sure.'

'And certainly not in the middle of the busiest day of the year.'

'Yeah, I guess I just didn't know how to explain to them why they couldn't talk to me about what they wanted at Lord Byron, because that's what they wanted to do when they saw me there.'

'I see.'

'And was there something in particular I was doing wrong? With them?'

'No. Well. Aside from vanishing for more than two hours without warning and without doing any actual work. No.'

'I get that. And I'm sorry. But that's not really what I meant. I meant if I wasn't doing a good job with Tim and Eric, and you felt the need to take over their account, I'd like to know what I was doing incorrectly?'

'It's not a question of right and wrong.'

'What is it a question of then?'

'Look, Camille. Let me think about it. Then I can write a whole bloody school report on the matter if that's what you want.'

'No, that's not what I want. I want to be talked to and treated like an equal, Holly. Like a human being.'

'Act like one, then.'

'A human being?'

'An *equal*. Sorry, hun. I thought you were someone who could appreciate constructive criticism when it was offered?'

'Offer some and I'll gladly receive it?'

'Camille, you look terrible. So I'm going to give you the benefit of the doubt and I'm not going to take anything you've said or done today personally, ok? I'm just going to write it off. Poof. There you go. I've forgotten all about it.'

'I don't want you to forget about it, Holly. It's important. It's my time. It's my ... *life*.'

'Omg. Look. Just go and get me my salad or something, ok? Grab some fresh air before you say or do something that you're going to regret. One day you'll thank me for that. So just go and get the salad and let's move on. Gosh. I'm famished! Oh, and let the girls know that the display boxes are in the car.'

'What?'

'The display boxes for that order. I've got them in the car.'

'Really?'

'And make sure they do a good job assembling that order. Then tell them to go home. They've been here long enough — oh dear. It's already 3.30pm! Doesn't the order go at 4pm?'

'It does, yeah.'

'Why on earth haven't they got the boxes from the car?!'

'Because nobody knew the boxes were in the car, Holly.'

'Careful with your tone, Camille. Go and get some air. Then come back and do your job.'

Camille is walking toward Lord Byron again and she's having what could only be described as an out-of-body experience. Her limbs are shadows of their former selves. Her mind is overrun with questions unanswered. Pains un-soothed. The rainbow spots have begun, but she's confusing them with the sunlight in her eyes. She's wafting past the bespoke homewares shop that opens at midday four days a week, and it's becoming clear that no one is coming to save her.

'Hi again. What can I get you this time?'

'Ah, a chicken Caesar salad.'

'Is that all?'

'Yeah. Actually, no. Umm ...'

'More coffee?'

And Camille is falling
fainting
everything is slowing down
Amy, the ceiling
the out-of-control black
eternity
a deep relaxation that cannot be stopped

'Mum?'

'Yes, Camille?'

'How did Grandpa Marcus die?'

'In a crash. You know that.'

'I know, but. How did he crash?'

'His car went into a tree.'

'Yes, but did he crash it? Or?'

'Or what?'

'Or did the car crash it?'

'I guess you could say ... both of them crashed it.'

'Did something go wrong in the car?'

'Not exactly.'

'Did something go wrong in Grandpa?'

'Yes. I suppose you could say that something went wrong in Grandpa.'

'Hey, Mum.'

'Yes, Camille?'

'What happens to people's phone plans when they die?'

Camille is standing in the clearing of a tropical rainforest. The greens around her are dark and lush. The soil beneath her feet is rich with biochar. The sound of rainbow lorikeets ricochets around her; soaring through the fragrant air that seeps into every cell as she breathes it in. It feels familiar here. Camille follows a path that winds its way between the ferns and through the frangipani and bamboo, which sounds like the sea when it shakes in the breeze.

It's late afternoon, and the smell of burning frankincense calls to Camille until she reaches a treehouse: it's timber, and on stilts, and surrounded by palm trees. Modern yet timeless. Californian yet Australian. There's a garden encircling it with plots of kale, and soft-wooded perennials, and herbs, and dahlias, and lilies, and figs, and lemons, and tomatoes, and silverbeet. There's a man watering. He's facing away from Camille, about twenty yards ahead, and he's wearing a wide-brimmed hat, jeans, and a long-sleeved shirt. His hair is grey.

Camille avoids him and moves in the direction of the stairs. The smell of frankincense guides her upwards. Wind chimes tinkle as she reaches a balcony where the remnants of lunch rest on the table: two oily plates, a large empty salad bowl, red-and-white striped cotton napkins, Moroccan tea glasses with wet mint in the bottom.

Someone is inside the house.

Camille approaches one of the windows. Through it, she can see an open kitchen with a distiller set up, and a lounge room with enormous cream couches, wooden floors, Persian rugs, hundreds of books, and a fluffy ragdoll cat lying in a patch of sun on the floor. There are ornate crystal bottles, and an apricot poodle drinking from a water bowl, and a woman sitting at a desk by a window looking out at the tops of the trees. She's turned away from Camille and she's leafing her way through a large book. The frankincense burns next to her. She seems to be trying to find something. She's very focused.

The poodle approaches the woman, and she gives it a pat while keeping her attention on the page. Her hair is long, and white, and held up by a tortoiseshell clip. She's wearing black denim overalls. Camille keeps thinking of Merlyn. Then she wonders if it's Jacqueline or maybe Holly. Then the woman turns, and Camille sees herself.

'Hey.'

'Mmm?'

'It's ok. You fainted.'

'Oh god.'

'We were tempted to call an ambulance, because your lips went blue, which was freaky! But. You were breathing, so. I decided to put you on your side. I had a feeling you'd wake up pretty quickly.'

'How long was I out?'

'Thirty seconds, maybe?'

'Oh.'

'Yeah, you were in the middle of ordering when you fell. Your eyes rolled back and shit. You're lucky you didn't hit your head on the way down. You sort of just ... sank. Withered like a bloody flower. Has that happened before?'

'Kind of.'

'Damn.'

'Yeah.'

'I think you just need something to eat.'

'Ok, thanks. I'm so embarrassed?'

'Don't be. I know it's weird, but. I've seen a lot worse than that in here.'

Lord Byron's superfood salad has multicoloured quinoa, and wilted spinach, and avocado, and pumpkin seeds, and a bright-orange Mexican salsa, and lightly blanched pieces of broccolini. Manny doesn't like quinoa with avocado, because everything becomes mushy. Camille likes mushiness, though. Mushiness is soft. And the green in the salad is really green. They also gave Camille heaps of avocado. Sometimes they don't. It really depends on the chef.

And while Camille was slowly eating her superfood salad, her period came. She felt that warm trickling sensation between her legs and in her underwear. Sometimes it's a phantom bleeding sensation. But when you know, you know — you know.

Camille felt stronger after finishing the salad. It nourished her deeply. Then she sat back in her seat and noticed how quiet and still Armadale is. Camille had no sense of how long she'd been away from Florals. Seamus took away the empty salad bowl and left a red rose on the table in front of her. He didn't say anything and she didn't look at him. Then, as Camille went to pick it up, she caught a glimpse of her reflection in the front window of LB. Her skin was glowing, and strands of hair around her face were stretching outwards, and reaching upwards toward the cosmos like a forcefield. Like electricity.

She looked inside Lord Byron, and Amy was at the coffee machine, and Seamus was leaning over the counter. They were laughing, and it was funny to think about what they'd laugh about together. Maybe they were laughing about Camille? And maybe that'd be ok. Maybe that'd be a nice contribution to have made to their day.

Camille is thinking about her menstrual cup back at Florals and about how nervous she gets when she has a lot to tell Manny. And does Amy expect her to pay for the salad? God. Of course she expects her to pay for it. Lord Byron isn't her lounge room now just because she fainted in it.

The business card. Camille is going to pay for her superfood salad with the business card. She's never put her lunch on the business card before. But today is different. And as Camille reaches into her pocket for the card, she finds the bottle of night-blooming jasmine. So she pulls it out, and she warms it in her hands, and she dabs its nectar on her wrists and neck. She closes her eyes, and inhales, and she takes comfort in the fact that she knows exactly what she needs to do.

'What took you so long, Camille?!'

'Umm.'

'This is a disaster!'

'Sorry.'

'Is that a rose from Seamus?'

'Ah ...'

'And where's my salad?'

'Ok, I don't know how to say this.'

'What? Say what?'

'I quit, Holly. I think I quit.'

'You *THINK* you quit?'

'I quit, Holly. Ok? I fucking *quit.*'

Both women fell silent.

'I knew this day would come. I knew this wouldn't work out. You can't even quit right! And it's *Valentine's Day* for Christ's sake.'

'I'm sorry, Holly. It's just that I really want to work directly with clients, and if that can't happen for me here, then. Yeah.'

'"Florals by Holly" is what you signed up for, hun. Not "Florals by Camille".'

'I know. I guess I see that now.'

'Well, good luck to you, then.'

'Thank you.'

'You're not even going to give proper notice?'

'No. I don't think so.'

'That'd be right.'

'Sorry.'

'And what about all of this crap on your desk? And on the walls? Are you going to take it with you?'

'Um. No. Do whatever you want with it, Holly. I'm going to say goodbye to Georgia and Alyce, and then I'm leaving.'

'Well, see ya, then.'

'And thank you.'

'For what?'

'Something. Probably a lot one day.'

Holly turned away and tried to act as if she was busy with something else, but Camille could tell that she was holding back tears. And the question that will linger in Camille's mind and heart for years to come is whether they were tears of rage or of sadness.

'Hey! What happened?'

'Sorry, I fainted.'

'Oh, shit?'

'Yeah, at Lord Byron. Then I quit.'

'What? No!'

'Yep. Just then.'

'How'd she take it?'

'Badly, I think.'

'Omg. I wanna quit!'

'Shut the fuck up, Georgia? This is my moment.'

'Sorry, sorry!'

'I'm really going to miss you, Camille. You held this place together. What the hell is going to happen now?'

'You'll both be fine.'

'Yeah, but whatever it is you're doing, *I'm there.*'

'Me too!'

'Ha! I don't know what I'm doing.'

'You wouldn't have done this if you didn't know what you were doing.'

'Maybe.'

'Shit. I wonder if Holly's going to offer me your job now.'

'Would you take it?'

'Camille, I'd take it in a heartbeat.'

Camille is floating down High Street, holding the rose from Seamus, moving past the by-appointment-only bridal shops, and the mirrored hair salons, and the perfumeries, and everything is different, because Camille is different.

She's noticing the people doing food shopping after work, and getting their nails done, and walking home, and to the station, and talking on the phone, and drinking their Happy Hour sav blancs, and carrying boxes of chocolates, and bouquets of Valentine's Day flowers, and she wants to say hi to them. She wants to ask them why they're doing what they're doing, and who they're doing it for. She wants to jump about, and to dance around — and there's no one to stop her.

There's a spin class happening upstairs at one of the gyms. Camille can hear it, because the windows are open, and there's techno music playing, and the thrum of wheels spinning, and a high-pitched voice screaming into a microphone: 'ok sexy *people*! Let's get *moving*! Let's get *sweaty*! Aren't we *happy* to be alive *today*!?' Camille has started running. She doesn't know why she's running, but she's laughing, and crying, and running down the street with her rose. Running through the world that is hers.

Camille has a window seat on the train home, which is packed. There are people standing all along the aisles looking at their phones. Everybody is waiting for something.

And through the crowded train, Camille can see her farmer friend up ahead. He's gazing out the window again. So Camille looks out her window to see what he's seeing, and the sun is setting. The sky is electric pink and pale blue, with plumes of violet, and streaks of gold — real Renaissance vibes, which Camille begins to absorb, and to become, before she glances around the train carriage and notices that no one else is looking at it. The golden light is falling upon them, but they can't see it.

♥

When Camille got home, Manny was sitting with his feet up on the table out the back, drinking a Bees Knees cocktail. He'd laid a Valentine's Day platter out before him and he's eaten some of it. He'd cycled into town and bought the best artichokes and Sicilian olives that he could find. He'd gotten blackberries to adorn the dark-chocolate mousse and he'd made tabbouleh using silverbeet from the garden.

Camille walked through the back door and stood in front of him.

'It's over.'

'What's over?'

'I quit Florals.'

'Holy shit. That's so great.'

'I know.'

Manny and Camille had sex in bed. He put on *Moon Safari* by Air. She lit damask-rose candles, and, initially, she worried that blood might go everywhere. Manny suggested they put towels down, but Camille didn't want to. If she bleeds, she bleeds. They can put fresh sheets on the bed before they go to sleep. She can clean the dirty sheets tomorrow. In fact, the idea of the dirty sheets soothed her. The sheets stained by the blood of today, This Day of All Days, this sacred day, this Day of Love, this *Valentine's Day*.

Manny was reluctant, but Camille insisted that putting towels down was less romantic than free bleeding. Then she pulled the petals from Seamus's red rose and she sprinkled them across the bed. She took off Manny's shirt, and he took off her dress. She touched his arms, hands, and fingers. He caressed her skin, sucked on her breasts. She felt his heartbeat and listened to her own. Then Camille wrapped herself around him and invited him in. She was a new person, and he was a new person, and they were a new couple, starting a new life. Camille orgasmed, and the remaining tension in her uterus dissolved into the ether, and gently shook the stars.

acknowledgements

I'd like to thank my other eye, Hector, for helping me through the writing of this book. Everything I do is better because of you.

I'd like to thank my parents, Tom and Debi, for their intelligence and care. It has been the fertile ground of my life and work and I'm eternally grateful.

I'd like to thank Nana — and all of my grandparents and ancestors — for watching over me.

I'd like to thank Marika and Scribe for guarding the soul of this book and for believing in me and my writing.

I'd like to thank Leah for her psychic notes.

I'd like to thank Liv for taking the time to talk to me.

I'd like to thank Casey for her insight.

I'd like to thank Needeya for coordinating the paperwork and for making me laugh.

I'd like to thank Lyndall and Jaqi for their guidance, wisdom, and reassurance.

I'd like to thank Katinka, Zero, Hamlet, and Rabbi for

guarding the sanctuary that is Hector's and my home and writing space.

I'd like to thank the water I drink, the food I eat, the air I breathe, and the land I stand upon.

And I'd like to thank all the women I know for being beautiful, and powerful, and for making impressions upon my heart and mind that will outlive me.